'Nobody in children's writing is producing
anything like this. It's electrifying.'
The Bookbag

'A modern classic.'
School Librarian

'Taut, intimate and wholly gripping . . .
a remarkable and riveting series.'
Books for Keeps

'A relentless and brilliant page turner.'
The Bookseller

'Stunning new thriller.'
Publishing News

'An addictive blend of paranoia and suspense.'
The Horn Book

'Sharply written without a wasted word.'
Irish Independent

'An intense, gripping story.'
Publishers Weekly

'Keeps readers on edge and turning
pages at breakneck speed.'
School Library Journal

'A gripping story.'
Julia Eccleshare *lovereading4kids.com*

'My heart felt as if it was a lot further up than its
normal position as I raced through *Blade*.'
Bookwitch

'Yet another captivating creation from Tim Bowler.'
Lovereading

'The tension is palpable and anyone who starts
this book will not be able to stop.'

BLADE ENDGAME

Other books by Tim Bowler

Blade
Enemies
Flight
Firestorm

Midget
Dragon's Rock
River Boy
Shadows
Storm Catchers
Starseeker
Apocalypse
Frozen Fire
Bloodchild
Buried Thunder
Sea of Whispers

BLADE

TIM BOWLER

UNIVERSITY PRESS

OXFORD
UNIVERSITY PRESS

Great Clarendon Street, Oxford OX2 6DP

Oxford University Press is a department of the University of Oxford.
It furthers the University's objective of excellence in research, scholarship,
and education by publishing worldwide in

Oxford   New York

Auckland   Cape Town   Dar es Salaam   Hong Kong   Karachi
Kuala Lumpur   Madrid   Melbourne   Mexico City   Nairobi
New Delhi   Shanghai   Taipei   Toronto

With offices in

Argentina   Austria   Brazil   Chile   Czech Republic   France   Greece
Guatemala   Hungary   Italy   Japan   Poland   Portugal   Singapore
South Korea   Switzerland   Thailand   Turkey   Ukraine   Vietnam

Oxford is a registered trade mark of Oxford University Press
in the UK and in certain other countries

First published as *Cutting Loose* and *Risking All* 2010
First published in this edition 2013

British Library Cataloguing in Publication Data

Data available

ISBN: 978-0-19-276363-1

1 3 5 7 9 10 8 6 4 2

Printed in Great Britain

Paper used in the production of this book is a natural,
recyclable product made from wood grown in sustainable forests.
The manufacturing process conforms to the environmental
regulations of the country of origin.

For Rachel
with my love

1

THE BRIDGE SLIPS from my grasp. I peer down at the river. It's yawning in the night, far below me, and I'm falling towards it like a wingless bird. Dead in my body, dead in my heart. Ready to die again.

Only I can't.

A weightless moment, an ecstasy of fear, then the vice closes round me, hooks my chest, jerks me upwards. Something hard slams into my back. The metal rails at the top of the bridge. My feet slither back on the ledge, skid off again.

The vice tightens, hauls me back against the top of the bridge. I hang there, whimpering, kicking my legs. Ruby's voice blares down at me.

'Chicken bastard!'

She's got me from behind. Must have reached through the rails just as I let go of 'em. Got both her arms under mine and they're locked round my chest. And now she's yanking me back towards the ledge.

'Chicken waster,' she mutters, 'chicken bloody—'

'Ruby—'

'Think killing yourself's going to sort everything?'

'Ruby—'

'Going to pay your debt to my daughter?'

'Ruby—'

'Well, it ain't! Cos jumping off a bridge don't pay no debt to Becky! Don't pay no debt to nobody!'

'Ruby!' I splutter. 'Ruby!'

She takes no notice, just goes on hauling me up.

'Let me go!' I scream.

'Don't tempt me.'

'I'm a piece of shit!'

'Yeah, like I don't know that.'

I kick my legs again, try to wriggle free. I don't want to live, Bigeyes. I don't deserve to. Becky died in the river. And she died cos of me. So I got to die there too. No question. I got to die there too.

I stare down at Mother Grime. Her black watery mouth's still open, waiting for me. I wriggle again, thrash about. Makes no difference. Ruby only tightens her grip, goes on pulling. I feel my feet clock back on the ledge. Ruby crabs her arms round my stomach, snags me hard against the rails.

I feel my hands close round the metal. Like they want to. Even if I don't.

I shut my eyes. No sounds from the bridge. No voices, no traffic. Just me and Ruby breathing hard, the river whispering below. Then Ruby's voice again, still raging.

'Think killing yourself's going to put you right, huh?'

I don't answer.

'Huh?' she snaps.

I open my eyes, stare down again. Mother Grime goes on flowing. I think of Becky's body, swallowed by water. How the grinks in the van shot her all those years ago, heaved her off the bridge to disappear for ever.

How it was my fault. Cos they were my enemies, Bigeyes, not hers. But she died and I lived. It's not right. Becky was my friend. My best friend ever. I should be with her, right now. Whatever her mum says.

Ruby tightens her grip, like she's picked up my thought.

'Still want to jump, right?' she fumes.

I say nothing. She leans her head close to the rails.

'Yeah, you do. You want to jump. You know why? Cos you're a coward. A slimy little coward. You think jumping off wipes your slate clean. Well, it don't. It's just the chicken way out. But I guess that's cool with you. The chicken way out. Cos it don't take no guts, huh? No responsibility, no—'

'Ruby—'

'Go and jump!' she bellows. 'If that's all you got. Cos I'm telling you—if that's the best you got for Becky, then you ain't worth piss. You want to top yourself? Go ahead!'

She lets go, slips her arms free.

'Or do something better. Your call.'

Sound of footsteps on the bridge. Ruby tramping away, heading for the north side. I watch her for a moment through the rails. She doesn't look back, not once. I want her to. But I know she won't. She'll just go on walking.

If I jump, she won't even notice.

I stare down at the river again.

'Mother Grime,' I murmur. 'You bitch.'

Look back at Ruby. She's disappeared from view, but she'll still be walking.

Still not looking.

'Bitch,' I murmur after her. 'Yeah, Ruby, you too.'

I climb back over the rail, drop down onto the bridge. Ruby's close to the north side now, trigging steadily on. I start to walk after her. Don't ask me why, Bigeyes, cos I don't know. She's the last person in the world I want right now.

And I'm the last person she wants.

But I keep walking, walking, walking.

Then I catch it. The sound of the motor. Coming from the south side. Doesn't sound like a problem. Shouldn't even be worried about it. Middle of the night, quiet time, but there's been other traffic, a bit anyway. This could be anyone.

Only it's not, Bigeyes. It's not anyone. It's trouble.

Don't ask me how I know.

I don't even need to look round. But I do. And it's what I thought. A van chunking over the bridge towards me, towards Ruby. Just like it did the day Becky got shot. And now here's her mum in just the same danger.

And once again—cos of me.

I scream at Ruby.

'Run for it! Run for it!'

I race down towards her. She's not running but she's turned and she's watching me hare across the bridge.

'Ruby! Run!'

She's still not running. She's stopped and she's just watching me. What's wrong with her? She must have seen the van steaming up behind me. There'll be grinks in it, just like there were with Becky. It's all happening again, like it did three years ago.

Sound of a shot.

Misses me, misses Ruby, but now she starts running, only—Jesus!—she's cutting the wrong way. Meant to be blasting off the north side but she's belting straight at me.

'Ruby, go back! Head for the alleyways! Other side of the main road!'

Engine's getting louder. Glance round. Van's close to the middle of the bridge now. Three gobbos in the front, one leaning out the window. Another shot.

Misses again.

I stumble on and here's Ruby bustling up.

'Ruby, for Christ's sake—'

She doesn't answer, just grabs my hand, pulls me over to the other side of the bridge. Van swerves across the road towards us. I'm praying for something else to slum up. Car, bus, taxi, whatever. But still nothing.

Van skews to a halt. Two of the gobbos pile out.

Ruby's still pulling me towards the edge of the bridge, and now I see where she's heading. The steps down to the wharf.

'Not down there, Ruby.'

She takes no notice, just goes on pulling.

'Ruby!'

She tugs me harder.

'OK, OK,' I mutter. 'I got what you want.'

She lets go and we pile down the steps. Feet pound behind us on the bridge.

This is a dronky idea, Bigeyes. I should never have let Ruby jam us down here. We'll never get away. The grinks are too fast, too strong, and they'll block the way back. And they got guns.

Shit!

First I get Becky killed, now it's going to be her mum. And Ruby was only trying to clip me clear of these grinks. I got to do my best for her. For Becky's sake too. Sound of feet above us.

Thump, thump, thump.

They're taking the steps in twos and threes. We got a lead but not much.

'Faster,' says Ruby.

2

BOTTOM OF THE steps and here's the wharf. Dimpy place to hide. We're separated from the bank by a small channel, got nothing to the left and just a short quay to the right with a few slaggy river boats and a big old motor cruiser at the end. No lights on any of 'em.

But we're not here to hide. I worked out Ruby's plan on the way down. She thought the alleyways up top are too far to get to, since the gobbos have got guns. So she's led 'em down here and now we got to belt back to the street, taking the steps up the other side of the bridge.

And lose the bastards on the way.

There's just a chance it might work. Both the gobbos are on this set of steps. I can tell from the sound of 'em. We might just be able to wig it up the others. I start to cut right but Ruby catches my arm.

Jesus, Bigeyes. Now what?

She's staring at the boats, and now she's pulling me off to the left. I glare at her. Heavy breaths above us, feet getting louder. Ruby glares back, pulls me harder, and now I get it. She's not heading for the other steps. She's slipping us round the back of these ones.

Another crap idea. Even worse than coming down in the first place. But we got no time to do anything else now. The grinks are almost down. I let her pull me round the base of the steps. She draws me in close to her, arm over my shoulder. I feel her breathing hard, her body warm against me.

Not acting like she's scared.

I'm telling you, Bigeyes, she's something, this woman. Might have made a dimpy choice coming down here but she's something. No wonder Becky had so much bottle. She got it from her mum.

Thump, thump.

Silence.

The grinks have hit the wharf. Only they're not moving. They're standing there, just hidden, other side of the steps. I glance at Ruby. She's pulled out her mobile.

Got one arm holding me close, and we're crouching in the darkness with those two grinks still standing there on the other side of the steps, and with her other hand she's texting.

Catches my eye, looks down again, goes on texting, sparks off a message, slips the mobile back in her pocket. Cool as a breeze. Not like me. I'm starting to breathe blood.

I can feel it pounding in my head. I got my hands moving inside my coat and they're squeezing the knives, just like they used to. Only it's not the same, not now. Cos I don't love the blades any more. I hate 'em. But it makes no difference.

My hands still find 'em.

Hold 'em tight. They're ready. Won't do much good probably. Least one of these grinks has got a gun. Maybe both of 'em. Maybe all three. But they haven't found us yet so we still got surprise on our side.

And that means a chance.

Ruby looks at me sharp. I try to read her face in the darkness. It's saying something, something I can't make out. And then I catch it. Something I recognize from the past. Cos it's something Becky used to have in her face.

The word no.

In her face, in her eyes.

No.

That's all.

No to what? Don't play thick, Bigeyes. No to everything. That's what it meant. Everything that's wrong, she meant. And there was plenty wrong back then. You bet there was. Right now it's the knives that's wrong.

Yeah, even here, with grinks ready to wipe us out, Ruby's felt my hands move inside my coat and she's guessed what they got, and her face is saying that word again, throwing it at me through the darkness.

No.

I feel my fingers ease.

Just a bit.

Sound of movement, other side of the steps. Slow, slow. They're not moving away. They're checking round and they're taking their time. They know we're still down here. They'd have rushed up the other steps by now if they thought we'd blasted out that way.

So much for Ruby's plan.

They'll check everywhere, including here.

And they're not stupid. One of 'em'll keep close to the steps. See what I mean? Shadow moving over to the right. Ruby's clapped it too. Pulls me closer to her, crouching even lower. Shadow hasn't turned, hasn't seen us yet. It's wandering down the wharf, stopping by each of the river boats, peering down.

And the other grink?

You guessed it. Bastard's still standing at the bottom of the steps. There's no way he's going to let us back up again. Easy piss. He stands here, guards these steps, keeps an eye on the other ones at the same time. Second gobbo goes looking.

Third gobbo up on the bridge checks down too. I'm guessing he can't see too good from up there, what with the bridge in the way, so we may just stay cute from him, but he's another problem we got to smack.

Shadow's stopped. Halfway down the wharf. Fixing one of the river boats. It's rocking in the swell. Sound of a cough from his mate. Still standing close to the bottom of the steps, just the other side of the brick. Check out the shadow again.

It's moving. Guy's clambering aboard the boat. Disappears from view round the back of the cabin. Only now Ruby's shifting too. Got a hand over my mouth.

Yeah, right. Like I'm going to suddenly blab a noise. Like I haven't spent my whole life ducking slime. I shake my head, scowl at her. She takes her hand away, grips my arm, edges me towards the side of the wharf.

Christ, no.

Effing water, just below us. I feel the old fear flick over me. Can't stop it. Ruby takes no notice. Maybe she doesn't realize, just thinks I'm freaking about the gobbos. Well, I am. I know what they can do, more than she does, maybe, but it's the water that's choking my head.

She's stopped again, still holding my arm, and now she's checking behind. I don't need to. I've checked already. First gobbo's still hidden behind the steps, other one's still on the boat. But we've moved out of the darkness and we're right at the edge of the wharf.

Moment the guy on the boat climbs back to the quay, he'll see us crouching here. I grab Ruby, try to push her back towards the steps. But she won't go. And now she's forcing me even closer to the water. Then I see it.

The ladder down the side of the wharf.

Into the river.

3

NO BOAT, NOTHING. Just Mother Grime, licking her lips. There's waves punching up against the wall. I shudder, check the ladder again. It's oily and covered in weed. I feel Ruby steer me towards it. I look round, catch her eyes.

Urging me.

Check the wharf. Shadow's appeared again, climbing back onto the quay. Hasn't looked this way yet. Could do any moment. Don't, you bastard. Go the other way. Check the other boats.

He doesn't. Just stands there, staring towards the other steps. He could look back any moment. His mate's still here. He's bound to check round. And then he'll see us. Ruby squeezes my arm again. And this time I move.

Over the edge of the wharf, grip the ladder. Metal's cold and wet and I hate the smell of the river hissing up at me. Clamber down, slow as I can, but not too slow cos Ruby's got to get down too, and she's got to be quick.

But here she is, climbing after me, quiet and sharp, like she's done this all her life. Stops just above me, looks down, nods me towards the river. Jesus, Bigeyes. I don't want to go any closer.

She nods again.

I try to control my hands. They're shaking bad now, and so's the rest of my body. Yeah, I know. I wanted to jump into Mother Grime earlier. But that was off the bridge.

I thought I'd die straight off from the impact, and if not that, then I reckoned I'd be so stunned I'd drown first gulp. But this is different. The water's over my feet now and it's creeping like blood.

Then I catch a new sound. Feet clumping down from the bridge. And voices. Only not from the steps but from the wharf. And it's not the two grinks. It's women. One of 'em bawls out.

'Who the hell are you?'

Raspy voice. Sounds like a hard shibo. I cling to the ladder rail, catch Ruby peering up at the top of the wharf, listening, like me. Second woman, another shibo. Tough, spitty.

'You looking for trouble?'

Third woman, same again. Mocking too.

'Cos if you're looking for fun, boys, you ain't getting none 'ere.'

Footsteps getting louder. And this isn't women. It's gobbos. Least three. Don't ask me how I know. They're muttering as they come. Hard slugs, same as the women. Now a new sound.

Running.

No prizes for guessing what that is. The grink by the stairs is wigging it. He's seen what's coming down and he's blasting off towards the other way out. His mate'll be doing the same. Yeah, he is. Listen to the women.

'Not stopping, then, boys?'

'Come on!'

'Show us what you got!'

I know what they got, Bigeyes. They got guns. So those shibos better watch their mouths. But it should be OK. The grinks won't use 'em down here, not for no reason. They'll pull 'em out if the shibos and these other gobbos get too close, but they're not looking for trouble.

They're looking for me. So as long as no one gets in their way, they'll keep the guns for later. More shouts from the shibos.

'Go on, boys!'

'Piss off!'

'Bastards!'

Sound of running up the other steps. Crane my head up. We're right under the bridge here and no one can see the ladder from up top. Don't think so anyway. Hidden from the road too, cos of the angle. So there's no way the grinks can shoot down at us, even if they know where we are.

But we're not out of danger.

No way.

I got these new dronks to think about. And the grinks won't go far either. They'll hang around nearby, wait for these nebs to go, then come back. They didn't see Ruby and me slam out, so they'll guess we're still down here.

Sound of an engine up above. The van, taking off.

Don't be fooled, Bigeyes. It's like I said. They won't be going far. They'll keep the top of the steps in view. So we're still in the grime. Ruby twists her body, leans closer.

'Now listen good,' she mutters. 'You wait here. On this ladder. You don't move, right? You stay here till someone come for you.'

'What you going to do?'

'Talk to my friends.'

I stare up into her face.

'Those guys up there,' I say. 'The ones just came down. You texted 'em, right?'

She shakes her head.

'I texted the women. They work on that old motor cruiser at the end of the wharf.'

'Work?'

'Yeah.' She fixes me hard. 'Work.'

Silence. Just the ripple of Mother Grime over the base of the ladder.

'Wait here,' says Ruby.

She starts to climb up the ladder.

'Thanks,' I call after her.

'Wait till someone come.'

And she's over the top and gone.

More silence, then a burst of voices from the gobbos.

'Hey, Rubes!'

'What's going on, babe?'

'You hittin' some shit?'

I cling to the ladder, listen. The shibos have joined the group too and Ruby's talking. But she's speaking low and I can't catch what she's saying. All I know is she's talking and they're listening. Like I told you, Bigeyes, she's something, that woman.

And I'll tell you something else. She's smart too. Cos listen—I just worked it out. She took one look at the alleyways off the bridge, knew we wouldn't make 'em, so she hit the steps.

First plan, I'm guessing. Lead 'em down here and lose 'em on the way up the other steps. But that was never going to work, cos the grinks came down too quick. Moment we hit the wharf I knew that. And Ruby knew it too.

But she had a second plan. Even as we were standing there, she was checking the old boat. Knew the shibos might be there, and maybe some other help. But there were no lights on. So she was cool enough to think of a third plan.

She knew that racing for the cruiser and taking a chance was a dimpy idea. If we found no nebs on board, we'd be trapped straight up. The grinks would have us on the boat and no way off. So she pulls me out of sight, texts the shibos, tells 'em to ring their mates and get 'em here quick.

Then thinks up Plan Number Four.

Slinks the two of us down the ladder. Case the help doesn't show and we got to blind it on our own. Some woman. Trouble is, thinking of Ruby makes me think of Becky again. I look down at the black water.

Feel the tears try to come.

Then realize the voices have vanished from the wharf. They're up on the far steps, moving higher, and now they're up on the bridge, and now . . .

They're gone.

I grip the metal rung. I'm starting to shiver. Mother Grime's slopping over my shoes and trouser bottoms. I spit down into her face, spit again, growl at her, climb up another two rungs, stop.

Ruby said to wait. I don't want to. I want to scramble up onto the quay and run my legs off. Before the grinks come back. But Ruby said to wait. So I got to stay put. I owe her that. Even though it seems like another bad idea.

Then I see a face looking down from the wharf.

Woman, about twenty-five. Black hair, zip eyes. Piercings all over—lips, nose, ears, brows. Christ knows what else she's got. No question who she is. One of the shibos from the motor cruiser.

She looks me over like I'm scum, then calls down to me. I recognize the voice. She was the one who taunted the grinks loudest.

'Let's go,' she snarls.

4

I CLIMB UP, punch a look round. No sign of any other nebs. Just me and the shibo standing here. I check her over.

Not wearing much but she's dramatic. Skimpy piece of nothing on top, even less underneath, but it's all black and leather, and there's bling bouncing every time she moves. Neck, wrists, ankles, fingers. Tats down her arms and round her middle. Snakes mostly.

She gives me a smile. It's like a winter's night. I cop a glint of more bling on her teeth and tongue. Then I realize it's not a smile. She's just opened her mouth to say something.

'Come with me.'

And that's it.

Turns and heads towards the old motor cruiser.

Or rather strides. Got some clash, this shibo, and too much spit for my liking. But I'm more freaked by the grinks. Like I told you, they won't have gone. And what's worse—they'll be ringing for backup.

Shibo goes on striding towards the boat. I follow, checking every way I can. Can't see any danger. Just the river boats rocking and Mother Grime licking past the wharf, and up above, the underside of Bogeybum Bridge. And up above that, a speckle of stars.

Shibo stops by the cruiser, fixes me.

'Get in the boat.'

I feel a shiver. Yeah, Bigeyes. You know about me and boats. And effing water. But I guess there's no other way. I start to climb onto the motor cruiser. Shibo clicks her tongue.

'Not that boat.'

She nods towards the stern.

'The dinghy.'

I check down towards it. Little shadow, bobbing on a line. Jesus, I hate these things. Even smaller than the one Bex put me in that time. And the water's more chippy than it was then. Don't shake your head, Bigeyes.

It is.

Look at those waves.

'Get in the dinghy,' snaps the shibo.

I trig down the quay, stop at the dinghy. Dronky thing. Looks like it wants to sink all by itself. I wish it bloody would. Oars already in it, and the rowlock things, or whatever they're called. I take a breath, sit down on the edge of the quay. Got to be a way into this dimpy thing.

Can't jump.

'Use the ladder,' calls the shibo.

She's still standing by the middle of the cruiser. Can't work out why she hasn't come down too. I check the quayside again. Yeah, she's right. More oily little rungs down the side of the wharf into the water.

I glance at her again.

Still not moving. Don't feel good about this, Bigeyes. First the water, now this woman trashing my head. She makes a huffy noise. I climb down the ladder, fumble into the dinghy. Look round. Shibo goes on watching me for a bit, then reaches out to the cruiser, knocks the side of the cabin with her fist.

Sound of movement inside, then a gobbo sticks his head out of a hatchway. Can't see his face but he's got dreads. About the same age as the shibo, I'm guessing. She leans close, mutters something. He twists round in the hatchway, checks me out, looks back at the shibo.

More muttering.

Now the shibo's coming over. Moves quick, confident. Down the ladder, into the dinghy, nods me towards the stern. I shift down there. She sits on the thwart, casts off, grabs the oars. Dinghy wallows. I clutch the side, feel my mind spin.

Shibo takes no notice, just eases us past the motor cruiser. But we're not heading out into Mother Grime. We're slipping in towards the wall, right under Bogeybum Bridge. And now we're creeping along it, down the narrow channel between the wharf and the bank.

I give the shibo a look.

'What we going this way for?'

'Was I talking to you?'

She's got a voice like a whip.

'Just asking,' I mutter.

She rows on, right under the bridge and close to the wall. Here's the ladder me and Ruby hung from. Looks spooky from the water, but not as spooky as the water itself. I'm dreading what's coming when we head out into the river.

But we're not doing that either.

We've stopped by the steps I came down with Ruby and we're sitting here in the darkness, oars dripping. I want to ask the shibo what she's waiting for, but there's no point. Her eyes tell me to keep quiet. So I keep quiet, and wait, still clutching the side of the dinghy.

Then I hear it.

The chug of the engine. Shibo looks back down the wharf and I do the same. The old cruiser's setting off. Two figures on her. The gobbo I saw earlier, now at the wheel, and a second gobbo, coiling rope.

No lights on still.

Just a ghostly shape, purring out into the river. Straight out, too, towards the south side, tracking the course of the bridge. I glance at the shibo. She cracks her eyes at me, like she doesn't like me looking at her, then dips her oars, and we're moving again.

Out from under the bridge, and now we can be seen from above. The shibo looks up and I do too, searching for grinks. Figures up on the bridge but it's hard to make 'em out in the darkness. No sign of Ruby.

One of 'em gives a nod.

Just a small movement but I catch it in the night. It's not to me. It's to the shibo. I can tell. Some kind of signal. Don't ask me what it means. Or the motor cruiser cutting off to the other side of Mother Grime.

The shibo rows on, along the line of the wall. There's a swell now, rolling across from the centre of the river and washing up the bank. Swish, swish, and back towards the boat. Makes me choke in my head. I'm squeezing the side of the boat and I'm trembling bad.

The shibo looks me over.

'What's up with you?' she goes.

'Nothing.'

'You're shaking.'

'I don't like water.'

'You scared of it?'

'No.'

'You is.'

She rows on, frowning. I check the wall. No faces looking down from the top, no sight of the road. I check the river again. Can't see the motor cruiser, but I can hear it. Sounds like it's a good way over the other side of Mother Grime.

I don't like this, Bigeyes. I was starting to trust Ruby. I mean, she got me off the bridge and away from the grinks. But into what? I don't like this shibo and I don't like the look of her mates.

We're moving closer to the wall. I check it over again. Maybe the shibo's just keeping us in the shadow. But I'm guessing it's more than that. Yeah, it is. See that? Steps cut into the wall. Shibo rows up to 'em.

'Get out,' she says.

I check over the side of the dinghy. Water's swirling over the steps, sucking in, sucking out. No way I'm putting my feet there.

'Get on with it,' mutters the shibo.

Yeah, like it's a whack getting out.

'Get on with it!' she goes.

I bung a scowl at her. Makes no difference. She just jerks her head at the steps. I climb over the side of the boat, gripping tight as I can. The water goes on churning round the brick.

I plant a foot on one of the steps, slip, gasp, catch my footing again, clutch the boat. I'm half-in, half-out, and the dinghy's pulling away from the wall.

'Christ's sake,' splutters the shibo.

Chugs her oars, eases the boat closer again.

'Now get out!'

I slither over onto the steps, fumble for something to hold. Feel a wave thump over my legs, crab me off balance. I start to tumble, flap my arms about.

'The rail!' shouts the woman.

I see it, grab it, squeeze it. I'm breathing hard, shaking worse than ever. I take a moment, look up. The steps lead all the way to the road. I take some more breaths, check round.

Shibo's already pulling back towards the wharf. Catches my eye, glares, rows on. I turn back to the steps, make my way slowly up. I got a bad feeling about this, Bigeyes. And I'm not talking about the water. I'm talking about what's waiting for me up top.

I want to pretend the shibo was just doing Ruby a favour. Getting me off the wharf and back to the road so I can wig it by myself. I want to pretend that was the plan all along. But it's not going to be that simple.

Don't ask me how I know.

I go on climbing, climbing, climbing. Yeah, like I thought. Here's the top of the steps. Here's the road. And here's the van.

Waiting for me.

5

ONLY I'M WRONG. It's waiting for me, yeah, but it's not the van. It's another van. Same colour, same type. But another van. Dirtier than the other one. Black gobbo standing outside it. About thirty. Hard dronk. No bling. Just muscle.

Doesn't like me. That's bung-clear.

But I don't like him much either.

'Get in the back,' he booms.

I don't. I'm checking the road. Bogeybum Bridge is off to the left, half-hidden by the bend in the road. Nothing to the right, apart from taxis rolling. No sign of grinks either way. But they can't be far. I look back at the gobbo.

No way I'm getting in the van with him.

He glowers.

'Ruby said get in the back.'

'She in there too?'

'No.'

'Then why should I get in the back?'

He says nothing. Just goes on glowering.

'You helped me,' I say. 'You and your mates. So thanks. But I'll take it from here.'

He pulls out a gun, points it at me.

'Get in the back.'

'That Ruby talking?'

'No,' he growls. 'That me talking.'

I get in. Nothing else to do. Two shibos in the back of the van. Black janxes, about Ruby's age. They just stare. Gobbo slams the door, walks round, climbs into the driver's seat. Nobody else with him in the front of the van. Turns round, stabs me with his eyes.

'You stay there,' he grunts. 'You got that?'

I fix him back.

'What else am I going to do, claphead? You got a gun.'

Gobbo narrows his eyes.

Shit, Bigeyes. I shouldn't have said that. What was I thinking of? He watches me, stretches out his arm, points the gun at my heart. I stiffen. Part of me wants to squirm backwards. Rest of me doesn't want to flinch.

I keep still, somehow. No point moving anyway. Nowhere to hide in here. Close by I feel the women watching. He gives a smile, squeezes the trigger—then pulls.

Gun gives a click.

Nothing more.

The shibos laugh. Gobbo does the same, a great bellow. Then throws the gun towards me. It slides along the floor of the van, thumps up against my leg. I don't pick it up, just stare back at the gobbo. He gives me a sneer, turns, starts the engine. And we set off down the road.

Towards Bogeybum Bridge.

Yeah, Bigeyes, now I'm confused. Can't work out what these nebs want. They're something to do with Ruby but that's all I know. They haven't hurt me yet and they've probably rescued me from the grinks. For the moment anyway.

But they don't like me.

Not one bit.

It's not just that shibo in the rowing boat. The gobbo in the front thinks I'm a dungpot. I can tell from his manner. And these two janxes in the back are staring at me like that shibo in the boat did.

Like I'm scum.

But maybe that's it, Bigeyes. Maybe I am scum.

Ruby should have let me jump. Do something better, she said. Yeah, but what? I've done all I can. Shunted Hawk with the gangster bojos. Given Bannerman all the bung about Hawk, told him where the stuff is, specially the backup hard drive from Hawk's computer. That's the thing he's got to do.

He's got to lift that backup drive.

It could finish Hawk. Might be the only thing that can.

So what else?

Eh? For a piece of scum.

What else but die?

Do something better. Yeah, Ruby. But what?

We're turning in the road, heading away from Bogey-bum Bridge.

Thank Christ for that. But I'm still scared, Bigeyes. Cos I still don't know who these nebs are or what they want. One of the shibos speaks.

'You're the shit that got Becky killed.'

So that's it. They know about Becky. Ruby must have told 'em, before she blasted off wherever she's gone. No wonder they hate me. But what does it mean? They've got me away from the grinks, and Ruby must have fixed that. But what do they want? And what does she want?

I offered her my life.

And that wasn't good enough.

So what else can I give her?

The shibos are still watching me. The one who spoke leans closer.

'You're the shit that got Becky killed.'

'You just said that.'

'I'm saying it again.'

Her mate stuffs a glare on me.

I stuff one back. I hate these janxes. I know they're right about Becky. And they're right about me. I am a shit. But it doesn't mean I got to be polite. Cos they certainly won't be.

Van rumbles on through the night. I can tell which way we're going without looking. Same as in the old city. I know my way too good round here to get lost. Even stuck inside a van.

But I can see anyway, through the windscreen. We've cut round Bogeybum Bridge, given it plenty of room, but now we're cracking towards Mother Grime again. I'm guessing the gobbo's taking us to the south side.

Told you.

We're clattering over the next bridge down from Bogeybum. Old Smokey. That's what I call this one. Always have done. Don't ask me why. I go on staring out through the windscreen. Sky's lightening, see? Just a bit. But what kind of a dawn will it be? And how many times have I wondered that?

I'll tell you, Bigeyes. Lots of times.

That's the crack of it. Dawn after dawn after bloody dawn. I'm fourteen, Bigeyes, and I've seen more dawns than I deserve to already. And every time I see one, I ask myself if it's going to be the last.

We're over Old Smokey now and hammering off south of the river.

I lean back against the side of the van, fix my eyes on the janxes. They're leaning together, murmuring stuff I can't hear. Rough women. Not as sparky as the shibo who rowed me off the wharf. She was spit-hard. But these two aren't much better.

We're turning left at the old power station.

Gobbo gives a cough, takes one hand off the steering wheel, pulls out a cig, lights it. Winds down the window, leaves it open. Cold air jets into the van. I pull my coat around me. Think of the knives inside. And then it hits me.

How come I only just thought of 'em?

The knives, I mean. How come I didn't think of 'em earlier? When there was danger. The shibo in the boat, these nebs in the van. How come my hands aren't already fixed on the blades like they used to be?

Yeah. Used to be.

Am I changing, Bigeyes?

Cos once upon a time I didn't need to think about the knives. I told you that before. My hands just went there by themselves. Only now, here I am in danger, and my hands . . .

They're just resting by my side.

And I haven't even thought about the knives.

Till this moment.

Maybe I'm cutting loose from 'em.

Or they're cutting loose from me.

Don't much care which. Long as it happens. Cos one thing I know, Bigeyes. Whatever I can do with a knife, it's not worth dog shit now. Won't save me. Not really. Not the part of me that matters anyway. The part old Mary found. And little Jaz.

And Becky. Sweet, beautiful Becky.

None of them ever needed a knife. So why do I?

I reach inside my coat, pull 'em out, hold 'em up. Look over at the shibos. They haven't even noticed. They've forgotten about me. Still naffing like before, into each other's ears, softer than the engine.

Gobbo hasn't noticed either. Takes a last drag of his cig, flicks the butt out of the window, lights another. Drives on, watching the dawn.

I stare at the knives again.

I've thrown 'em away before, Bigeyes. And every time they've come back. But maybe this time'll be different. Maybe this time I'll really cut loose. And be free.

I throw 'em towards the front of the van. They clunk on the floor, slide along it, disappear under the driver's seat. The janxes stop talking, fix me for a moment. Gobbo does the same in his mirror. Then back again, like before.

Janxes go on talking.

Gobbo goes on smoking. And watching the dawn.

They don't even know what I threw. And they don't care either.

I ease myself down, curl up on the floor of the van. Doesn't matter where these nebs are taking me. I don't give two bells any more. Something hard's pressing into my side. Feel round with my hand. It's the gun, digging into me. Scrab it tight, chuck it after the knives.

Close my eyes.

Sleep.

 WAKE. OR RATHER get woken. Gobbo's voice, blasting over me.

'Get up!'

The black gobbo, leaning close. Breath stinks of cigs.

'Get up!' he bawls.

'Piss off!'

A hand clips me on the cheek, does it again. I blink my eyes open, spit up at him. I was dreaming of Becky. Sweet, darling Becky. And now this jerk's gone and—

Whap!

He clips me again, harder. Then growls into my ear.

'You don't spit at me. And you don't tell me to piss off. You don't never do that.'

Grabs me by the collar, yanks me up till I'm sitting. I stare at him, still clutching the picture of Becky in my head, and her smile, her beautiful smile. Only now it's fading and I got this bum glaring at me instead. Van's stopped, back door's open. He's standing outside it, leaning in, the two shibos just behind him.

And Ruby.

Behind them.

'Don't hurt him,' she says.

'Why not?' mutters the black guy. 'He got no manners. He got your girl killed. He don't care about nobody. Not you, not Becky—'

I feel my fist snap out. Can't stop it. Moment he said Becky's name.

I hit him hard in the face. Doesn't hurt him but it takes him by surprise. He gives a roar, pulls back his arm, fist clenched. Ruby yells.

'Seth!'

It's not a request. It's a command. No question. And the gobbo obeys it.

Just.

He's got his fist back ready, and it's shaking, shaking. His body's shaking too. He's got his eyes fixed on me, his mouth spitting hate. He wants to kill me. He wants to slam me into the darkness so I never come back.

'Seth.'

Ruby again, quieter this time. She comes forward, pushes between the two shibos, slips a hand round the big guy's fist, eases it back down. Then leans in to the van, fixes me. And slaps me hard in the face.

'Get out of the van,' she mutters. 'And keep your mouth shut.'

I get out of the van. Have to push round the black gobbo, cos he's not moving. But he doesn't hurt me. Just glowers into my face. I step back from him, and the others, check round. We're in a garage, multi-storey, basement level, I'm guessing.

Nobody else here. Plenty of space, just a couple of other motors, empty, and this van. Look back at Ruby and the others. Just the four of 'em. Seth, Ruby, and the two shibos.

Watching me.

Sound of an engine. I check round again. Car pulling in, wheels screaming. Two black guys in the front, shibo in the back. The one who rowed me off the wharf.

Just what I don't need.

They squeal up, stop, get out.

Join the others.

All watching me.

'Let's go,' says Ruby.

The others turn towards the exit. Ruby stays put, her eyes on me.

'That means you,' she mutters.

I walk up to her.

'And keep your mouth shut,' she says.

I follow her, through the exit, up the steps. I was right. Basement level. We cut up the stairway, nobody talking. Silence feels strange, kind of threatening. Don't know why, Bigeyes, but it's like they're all waiting for me to speak.

Keep your mouth shut, Ruby said. But I don't think she means that. Keep it shut now, yeah, but not later. There's talking to come, and it's coming from me, and they all want to hear it. Don't ask me how I know. And till they get to listen, nobody's going to speak.

So the silence goes on.

As we walk.

Out of the multi-storey, round the back of the shops, through the estate, out the other side. I know this place, Bigeyes. Not well, I mean not really well, like I know the rest of the Beast. We're way south here, right on the outskirts of the bastard. But I've been here a few times.

Scragland.

That's what I call this area. Dronky shops, dronky estates. Nobody's got any jippy round here. We're cutting left, round the little park, out the other side. Day's waking up. Don't know what time it is.

Haven't seen a clock and I'm not going to ask any of this lot. No sun in sight. Just a grey, chilly sky. Far off in the north I can feel the Beast snorting. Even out here I got his smell choking me, like Seth's ciggy breath.

Turning left, down a little street. Terrace houses, crumbly and old. Sound of televisions on, radios, man shouting at a kid in one of the kitchens. We trig on past, now right, through a gate, through a walled garden, bin-bags and rubbish all around, and up to the back door of a house.

It opens as we reach it.

And there's another gobbo standing there.

Old guy, black like the others. Don't know him but he looks familiar. Then I guess it.

'Hello, Poppa,' says Ruby.

He doesn't answer. Just stands there, looking out. Nothing wrong with his head. I'm telling you, Bigeyes. He's got all his fizz. I know why he's not moving. He's looking out, looking for one thing.

Me.

We fix eyes.

And I look down. It's no good, Bigeyes. I just can't do it. I can't look Becky's grandpa in the face. Specially now, when I'm not prepared. I didn't know she had a grandpa. She never told me. But then, you know what?

That's kind of how it was.

I'm only just getting that now.

We never really talked about her. Yeah, yeah, we talked about what she was doing at school. But that's only cos she was trying to help me. She loved school and she wanted me to go with her. So we talked about that.

Or she did.

But we never talked about her. Not properly. We only ever talked about me. Me, me, bloody me. And she was cute about that. You know why? Cos all she ever wanted to do was help me. Get me out of trouble, make me better, make me worth something.

Stead of what I am now.

Worth nothing.

I look up. I make myself. And there's the old gobbo still watching me. His eyes don't move. And I know he knows. About how Becky died. Ruby's rung him, texted him, whatever. He knows. He must hate me so bad.

'You better come in,' he murmurs.

Deep voice, quiet, sort of thoughtful.

They walk in, slow, nobody talking. And it's just like before, Bigeyes. Like they're waiting. For me. Yeah, that's right. It's me got to break the silence. Only not yet. Not till they're ready for it.

And they'll show me when they are.

They file through, into the house.

I follow. I don't want to. And I could get away easy. I'm last in and nobody's looking back at me. But I walk on. I know I got to. Into the lounge and there they are all standing there.

Old Poppa, Ruby holding his hand. The big guy, Seth, still raging at me. The two janxes from the back of the van, the hard shibo with the piercings who rowed me off the wharf. Miss Spikyface. And the two new dronks.

Yeah, and now I recognize 'em.

The motor cruiser. One at the wheel, the other coiling rope. And now that bit's starting to make sense. The old boat chuffing off into Mother Grime. It was a decoy. They sent me in the dinghy with Spikyface and she got me up the steps to the van. But they used the motor cruiser to distract any grinks who might be looking.

Ruby made her way here on her own.

Or something like that.

Whatever.

I'm here. And these nebs are here. And Jesus, Bigeyes. Someone else is here. Someone I just noticed behind me. On the mantelpiece.

Becky.

Oh, Christ.

Same photo as Ruby's got in her little shrine at home. Same smiling face.

I look away. Can't bear to see it. And feel the guilt.

Poppa sits down on the sofa, Ruby next to him, hand on his knee. The others sit down too—Spikyface in the armchair, dronks on the floor, janxes flopped against 'em, one either side.

Nobody moves. Nobody lights a cig, makes tea. They just watch me. And wait. I'm still standing. I glance at Becky, feel the guilt again. Sit down on the floor, in front of the old man.

He looks back at me and there's something in his eyes. Something . . . I don't know . . . something I haven't seen much in my life. A piece of Ruby, yeah, and Becky, but it's not just that. It's something else. I've seen it in Jaz too. And Mary.

It's something they all got.

And I haven't.

Am I imagining this, Bigeyes? No, I'm not. It's there. It's definitely there. That . . . thing they all got. That special . . . thing. And I know I got to hold onto it. Cos I might never see it again.

I don't want to call it love, cos it's not love. But I'll tell you one thing.

It's the opposite of hate.

The old man reaches out, takes Ruby's hand.

Fixes me with his eyes.

'It's time to talk,' he says. 'About Becky. And those men who are trying to kill you.'

7

SO I TALK. And I do something I never meant to do. Certainly not to these nebs. I tell the whole story. Yeah, Bigeyes. The whole effing lot. More than I ever told Bex or Bannerman or anybody.

It just comes flooding out. Like I can't stop it.

And suddenly I don't want to.

I tell 'em about the home I first lived in, how I got found outside. And what happened to me inside, even though I can only imagine it. I tell 'em about burning the place down, running away, getting into trouble.

Hawk getting hold of me. What he trained me to do. Killing, I mean. And how good I was. That's right, Bigeyes. I give 'em numbers. I count 'em out, all the dead dronks. And I give 'em Hawk's name. Yeah, you bet. I want 'em to know.

Lord Haffler-Devereaux.

I say it twice. I spell it. I say it again. I tell 'em what he looks like, how he talks, how he thinks. What he likes to do with small boys. What he did with me.

I tell 'em about Becky. How I loved her, how I still love her, how I'll always love her. I tell 'em about seeing her die, running away, playing dead in the old city. I tell 'em about Trixi and the troll-gang. And Mary. The bungalow, the grinks catching up with me. I tell 'em about Bex, and little Jaz.

Riff finding me, Dig getting killed.

And Jaz taken.

Coming back here, to the effing stinking Beast. Kidnapping Hawk's boy, getting Jaz back. And then seeing her taken away for ever. Like it's meant to be. Like it's always meant to be. Cos that's how it is, Bigeyes. Everyone I care about gets taken away. Becky, Jaz, Mary. Everyone.

I go on talking. No one stops me. They just listen. I talk about the Game, the power play that's smashing up this world. I talk about the slimeheads at the top and the low-life underneath. I talk about Ezi and Spit, how I cranked up Nelson and the other gangster bojos.

How I got in touch with Bannerman. I tell 'em what I told him, what I wrote down for Ezi and Spit, what the gangster bosses round the Beast now know. I tell 'em about Pink getting shot. And how there's going to be more. Loads more.

Then suddenly I stop. I look up at the photo of Becky.

And burst into tears.

I didn't mean to. But it's like the talking. It just came flooding out and now I can't stop it. I close my eyes, dip my head, hug my knees into my chest. I feel my body shake as I howl into the dark.

Don't know how long it lasts.

Just feels like it's for ever.

When I open my eyes again, they've all gone. I'm still hugging my knees but I've stopped crying, stopped shaking. My eyes are blurry with tears. I wipe 'em with my sleeve, sniff hard. Feel a hand touch the top of my head.

Then go.

It's Ruby. Can't see her but I know it's her. Standing behind me. I look round, peer up at her. She's frowning, lips tight together. I wipe my eyes again.

'I'm sorry,' I murmur.

The tears bubble back.

'I'm sorry.'

I squeeze my eyes tight as they'll go. The hand touches my head again, hesitates. I feel it wanting to go. I reach up, grab it, hold it there.

Go on crying.

The hand stays. It doesn't stroke.

But it stays.

I hear 'em come back in the room. Some of 'em anyway. I don't bother looking. Too busy crying. But I'm easing off now. Not sobbing any more, just whimpering like Hawk's kid when he was curled up in the car and thought I was going to kill him. Don't ask me why I'm thinking of Damien at a time like this.

Ruby's hand goes. I open my eyes again, look up. She's walking back to the sofa. The two janxes have come back and the dronks who rolled up in the car. Nobody else.

Sound of a radio playing down the corridor. Clattery kitchen noises, Poppa's voice, low and slow. A sharp, snappy laugh. Got to be Spikyface. Throaty chuckle from Seth. Poppa's voice again. Can't clap what he's saying.

I look over at Ruby. She's sat down on the sofa. Other four are sprawled on the floor again. Steps in the corridor. Seth and Spiky come in. Ruby glances up at 'em.

'He sent us back,' says Spiky.

'Said he don't want no help,' mutters Seth.

Ruby doesn't answer. Just watches 'em sit down on the floor.

Then turns to me.

'So what was his name?' she says. 'Or don't you know it?'

She's narrowed her eyes and she's checking me close. I know what she wants, Bigeyes. The guy who shot Becky. And yeah, I do know his name. You bet I do.

The clattering goes on in the kitchen. Radio still playing but Poppa's changing channels. I hardly listen. All I hear is the silence in this room, and my own fear shrieking inside it.

Becky looks down from the mantelpiece. I look back and there's that thing in her face. The opposite of hate. The thing that can't be love. I look back at Ruby.

'Ricky Dean,' I tell her. 'That's the guy's name. But they all called him Milky. Cos of his hair.'

She stiffens, looks round at the others.

'You heard of this guy?'

They shake their heads. She looks quickly back at me.

'You got an address?'

'It's no good you going—'

'I'm not going no place.' She glares at me. 'I'm sending the police round.'

'Ruby—'

'Just cos it happened three years ago don't mean—'

'Ruby—'

'Don't mean it's too late for justice—'

'Ruby, he's dead.'

Silence again. I feel 'em all staring at me. Clattering sounds come back. Some part of me picks up that the radio's gone off. And there's footsteps in the corridor again. Moving slow.

'He's dead, Ruby,' I say. 'Cos I killed him.'

She breathes in sharp. Poppa appears in the doorway, holding a tray. Walks over to me, bends with an effort, rests it on the floor. I look down at it. Tatty old thing, stained and peeling. Chipped blue plate on it with sausages, beans, eggs, mush. Knife and fork. Glass of orange juice. Napkin in a little red holder.

Got Becky's name on it.

Oh, Jesus.

Poppa nods me towards the food.

'Eat,' he murmurs.

I pick up the knife and fork. Don't touch the napkin. Can't do it. Feel like it's wrong. Whatever the old man means by it. I start eating. Poppa doesn't move away.

Clears his throat. Deep, slow sound, like the way he talks. I look up at him, snap the meaning from his eyes.

But it's no good. I still can't do it.

He starts to bend down. Big effort like before. I can't let him do this.

'OK,' I say quickly.

He stops, halfway down, his eyes still on me. And there's something in 'em makes the guilt even worse.

'OK,' I say again.

And I pick up the napkin holder. He straightens up, rubbing his lower back. Stands over me, looking down. Big, sad eyes, same as Ruby's. I pull the napkin out of the holder, feel the tears splutter inside me again.

'Eat,' says the old man.

He's still watching me. I'm still watching him. I take a breath and somehow the tears stay back. Poppa moves off, sits down on the sofa next to Ruby. She rests her head on his shoulder. I spread the napkin on my lap, smooth it out, gentle as I can. Put the holder back on the tray. Look up at Becky's photo.

Start eating again.

Room stays quiet. No one talks till I've finished and pushed the tray aside. Then Poppa leans forward.

'There been more violence in the city,' he says.

8

THE OLD MAN doesn't hurry. Takes his time with the words. Tells us what he heard on the radio before we got here, what he heard while he was cooking.

First up, the porkers have found the diamonds and art stuff I left in my hiding places back in the old city. Bannerman must have got 'em onto that bung-quick cos Poppa heard it on the news at six this morning. Massive haul of stolen artefacts, worth a fortune. Jesus, Bigeyes, they got it.

But the Beast's the place where it's really ripping up.

Three more shootings. No names mentioned but it sounds like high-level dronks. I'm guessing the top three spikes on Ezi's list. Nelson won't have cracked them on his own. He'll have needed help from the other gangster bosses, so that means Fitz and Spice at least are in it, and maybe some of the other bojos, and all their dregs.

Hawk'll know he's in a fight now.

But it won't be enough on its own. The bastard's too smart. The moment this stuff hit the news Hawk'll have pulled up the drawbridge and hidden anything that could shunt him.

No, Bigeyes.

It's down to the backup hard drive from Hawk's computer.

If Bannerman's lifted that too, we got a chance.

Poppa goes on talking, in his soft, slow voice, rolling out the words he's snagged from the radio bulletins. Police investigation, criminal network. Still no names mentioned. Then I catch one.

Mine.

And see Poppa looking straight at me again.

'Every news bulletin,' he says, 'your name get spoken. They all talking about the boy called Blade.'

The others look round at him, then at me.

Poppa narrows his eyes.

'It's time to choose,' he says.

I know it is, Bigeyes. And I know exactly what he means. Cut loose from knives, from killing, from everything I've been. Or stay the same. And go on suffering even more. But Poppa doesn't put it that way.

'You can come with me,' he says, 'and we go find this Mr Bannerman. Or you can just go now. Walk out the door. Wherever you want to go.'

The old man pauses, goes on.

'And I go talk to Mr Bannerman by myself.'

Silence. I feel the others watching me hard. But I keep my eyes on Poppa. I know what he wants, Bigeyes. He wants me to go with him. He doesn't want me to choose the head start.

Somebody's mobile chinks. I see Ruby reach into her pocket, check a text. Poppa goes on watching me. And you know what, Bigeyes? Suddenly it's like Mary's watching me too, sitting there with the old man, urging me to do what he wants.

I glance up at Becky.

Yeah, sweetheart. It's what you want too, isn't it?

It's what everyone wants.

I look back at Poppa. His face is so grave. He shakes his head.

'No point running no more,' he murmurs. 'You done some bad and you got to face up to that. But you done some good too. You must not forget that. So let's you and me go find Mr Bannerman.'

Before I can answer, Ruby cuts in.

And the panic in her voice makes us all sit up.

'Bex is in trouble.'

I stare at her.

'What's happened?'

'I give her my mobile number. When you first left her with me. Made her write it down. Case she ever needed it.'

'But what's happened?'

'She just sent me a text. It's written bad but I worked it out.'

'What does she say?'

'She been beat up and she's run away again. Got some guys looking for her. She's scared out of her head.'

'Where is she?'

'Hiding in my back garden. Says she can't get in the house cos she can't find the spare key.'

Ruby frowns.

'But I told her where it is. I showed her. Before she ran off.'

She's freaked out, Bigeyes. She's forgotten where the key is cos she's too choked to think. We got to help her, got to do something. Ruby's already on her feet.

'Poppa, you take care of Blade. Rest of us got to go look for Bex.'

'I'm coming with you,' I say.

'No, you ain't,' says Ruby. 'Poppa just give you two choices. And coming with us ain't one of 'em.'

'I'm still coming.'

Ruby takes no notice, turns to the others.

'Seth, get the van. Wait for us by the shops.'

'What about our motor?' says Spiky.

'Best we all go in the van,' says Ruby. 'Poppa's going to need the motor to drive Blade to the police station.'

'I'm not going to the police station,' I say. 'I'm coming with you.'

I feel 'em all turn, fix me. But most of all I feel Poppa's eyes. They're the only ones not angry with me. But I'm forgetting Becky. Her eyes aren't angry either. They never were.

'I got to come with you,' I say. 'For Bex's sake. Cos I can help her. I can tell her about Jaz being all right. Bex'll want to know. That little girl means everything to her. Everything in the world. And she'll want to hear it from me. Cos I saw Jaz face to face. You got to let me come. For Bex's sake.'

Ruby frowns, then bungs a glance at the others.

'Go get the van and the motor.'

They crash out of the room and suddenly there's just me, Poppa and Ruby left. And Becky, watching quiet. Ruby turns away, punches a number into her mobile, put it to her ear, waits.

Poppa's eyes settle on me again.

But he says nothing.

Ruby gabs into the phone.

'Bex, it's me, Ruby. Listen, if you get this message, we're coming, OK? You're going to be fine. We're on our way. And Blade's with us and he's coming too. He's going to tell you all about Jaz. Cos she's cool, yeah? She's safe. She's with good people and she's safe. So we're coming and we're going to look after you. Now listen good. The key—it's under the brick just behind the bin. You got that? Under the brick. Just behind the bin. Now you go get that key and you let yourself in, then you lock the door again and go upstairs to the bedroom, and you wait for us there. Don't turn the lights on and keep away from the windows. You got that? We're coming now and I'm keeping my mobile on, case you want to ring. Be strong, girl. You're going to be fine.'

She hangs up, turns back to us, frowns again.

'Am I doing this wrong, Poppa? With Blade, I mean.'

She peers into his face like a small girl.

Like Becky almost.

Yeah, like Becky.

The old man takes a long, slow breath. Like he's counting out the ones he's still got left. Then looks straight at me.

'Only Blade knows if this is right or wrong,' he says.

There's another silence. Too deep to feel comfortable.

'I'll come straight back,' I say. 'I promise I will. I'll come straight back. And go with you to Inspector Bannerman.'

I look him hard in the face. I want him to believe me. I want that so much.

Poppa looks back.

And says nothing.

9

VAN RUMBLES THROUGH the grey morning.
I'm slumped in the back next to Ruby with Spiky sitting
opposite. Seth's driving like before. Nobody with him in
the front. The janxes have gone in the motor with the
two dronks.

Can't say I miss 'em.

Only problem is I got Spiky fixing me with those eyes.

Ruby's trying Bex's mobile again. But she's still getting
voicemail. Leaves another message, hangs up. I'm trembling. Can't think straight. All I got in my head is Bex.

I can't crack this, Bigeyes. This . . . caring. Cos it's back
again, right? Caring about Becky, Jaz, Mary, that's cute. I
get that. But caring about Bex? Of all people. I didn't
think she meant anything to me. But she does.

I can't bear to think of her shivering in Ruby's garden.

I just want to get to her quick. I want to tell her about
Jaz. Cos you know what? That'll pick her straight up.

She'll fight back then. She was never busting with grit. You seen that for yourself. She's not yellow, like Trixi used to say. I found that out bung-quick. There's no way that girl's yellow.

But she's not busting with grit.

So I'm going to tell her about Jaz. And you just watch her get better. She'll be fizzing when she's heard about Jaz. And I'll tell you something else, Bigeyes. I'm going to get Bex sorted, make sure Ruby's got her safe, then I'm heading back to Poppa. And I'm going to prove to him I meant what I said.

We're going straight to Bannerman.

And I'm going to give myself up.

'You was brave,' says a voice.

I look up, startled. Spiky's watching me from the other side of the van. Her eyes seem to prick the inside of my head.

'What you told us about kidnapping that boy,' she says. 'And getting Jaz back. You was brave.'

I stare at her, not sure what to say.

If anything.

She watches me a moment longer, then turns her head.

We drive on, heading towards Ruby's district. That's right, Bigeyes. The Den, remember? One big shithole. Least we got muscle with us this time. But I'm still worried sick about Bex. She found her way to Ruby's house. That part of her's still working.

But what's happened to her? Beaten up, she said. Question is—how bad and who by? And who's after her now?

Spiky calls out suddenly.

'Seth!'

'What's up, babe?'

'Who left them knives there?'

'What knives?'

'Under your seat. I can see 'em from here.'

'They're mine,' I cut in.

Spiky fixes me again. I catch Seth's eye in the mirror too. I look down.

'They're mine,' I say. 'Only they're not.'

'What you talking about?' says Spiky.

'I threw 'em away.'

'You what?'

'I don't want 'em. You can have 'em if you want. There's a gun under there too. Seth's gun. Take the lot.'

I look up, drill her eyes. 'Got a problem with that?'

'No,' she says.

'Good.'

I look away. Can't face her. Can't face any of 'em.

And I can't face the knives. Not any more. Not ever again.

I feel Ruby take my hand. I flip my head, fix her. And there's that thing in her face again. The thing I want so much. The opposite of hate. I feel a shudder, stare into her eyes, try to think of another way of saying sorry.

A better way. But it's no good. I just can't.

She lets go of my hand, touches my cheek.

Turns away too.

Van thunders on, closer to the Den, into the Den. Ruby's calling directions now, taking us there by a dronky route. But I know what she's doing. She's making sure we don't get clapped too easy. Cos there's guys out there, Bex said.

Hunting her.

And we don't want 'em hunting us too.

Seth's slowing down and we're all watching out. Ruby's up in the front now, next to the big guy.

'Left,' she mutters.

Seth turns left, chunks through the gears.

'Not too fast,' says Ruby.

He stays in third, lets us rumble down. I know where we are. You bet. And Ruby's playing it just right. We'll come at her house from the back. I'm guessing she'll take us down Regency Road, stack the van and trig us through the estate.

'Left again,' she says.

Told you, Bigeyes. Down Regency Road, on to the end. Seth's braking.

'Pull over,' says Ruby. 'By the wall.'

He pulls over, turns off the engine. We don't get out. Ruby's on her mobile again. Tries Bex's number first. Voicemail again. Tries another number. I'm guessing the dronks who went in the motor with the two janxes.

'You got there?' she goes.

Silence while she listens.

'OK,' she says. 'Meet us where I said.'

Hangs up, looks round at us.

'Let's go.'

Out of the van and here's the back of the shopping precinct. Not too many nebs out yet. Couple of old dunnies pushing trolleys. Girl in school uniform. Stuffs a shiver round my heart cos it makes me think of Becky.

Same uniform, same school.

But I can't think about that now and Ruby's striding on anyway. I can feel her fretting, like I'm doing. Bex is close but Christ knows what state she'll be in. She might even be dead.

She hasn't answered her phone.

And you'd think she'd be checking. She should have got Ruby's messages by now. I can feel my heart pounding as I speed up. But I'm still glancing round. It's not just Bex who's in danger here. I got to think of myself too. Even with these three for support.

No sign of the nebs from the motor. I didn't see Ruby fix anything with 'em. Maybe she texted while I wasn't looking. She did something anyway. Cos suddenly here they are, waiting on the other side of the precinct.

The two dronks anyway.

The janxes have disappeared.

'You done what I told you?' says Ruby.

Guy with the dreads answers.

'We left the girls outside the house.'

'Where exactly?'

'Over the street, down the little lane. Like you said. They can see the house but they're out of sight. They'll text if any shit turns up.'

'Any sign of Bex?'

Guy shakes his head. Seth flexes his muscles.

'Let's go,' he grunts.

'Wait,' says Ruby.

She holds out a hand, stops him. And now she's looking round. Yeah, Bigeyes, and I know why. She's got that same feeling I got. A feeling I've had many times.

When you know something's wrong but you can't see it.

10

WE'RE ALL CHECKING round now. No sign of trouble. Nebs coming and going but they're all muffins so far. Can't work out what's wrong. But that's often how it is, Bigeyes. You can't work it out. You just know.

Ruby catches my eye.

And something passes between us. Something I haven't seen before. Not from her anyway. She's checking what I got. What I'm picking up. Cos she knows I crack stuff most nebs don't. She's watching me close, looking for anything I can give her.

Or maybe just reassurance. That she's playing this cute. I guess it's respect. But that's not what matters right now. Bex is what matters. Ruby's still watching me.

'What you getting?' she says.

'Nothing. But I don't feel right.'

She doesn't answer, just goes on checking round. Couple of kids run past, gobbo walking a dog. Three dunnies, naffing. One looks us over as they plod by. Ruby watches 'em go, turns to us.

'Let's go,' she mutters.

We trig on, over the car park, down the alleyway, round the corner to where the back gardens start. Ruby stops, checks again. We're all flicking round, watching for scum.

But nobody's here.

Alleyway's deserted.

Apart from a cat. Then that wigs it too.

I run my eye down as far as the street. No sign of movement there, no cars even. We walk on, slow, checking as we go. Even Spiky looks nervous. I glance at Seth, just in front of me. He looks bigger, meaner, and so do the two dronks in front of him. I got to admit I'm glad they're here.

But I still don't feel right.

Gate on our left. First of the back gardens. We walk past it, past the next, and the next. And here's Ruby's. I stare at it. Feels weird, Bigeyes. You know why? I'll give you another confession. Yeah, yeah. Another one.

I waited out here once.

For Becky.

That's right. Just once. When she wasn't supposed to be seeing me. She sneaked out in secret just to talk to me. We didn't go off anywhere. She had homework to do and didn't have time. And she felt guilty not telling Ruby.

So I waited for her here.

And she slipped out and we slumped down against the wall.

And talked soft, so no one could hear us.

Then she went back in.

I remember sitting here after she'd gone. Just sitting and dreaming about her. She never knew. Cos I never told her. She'll have thought I just ran straight off. Back to my dirty life of crime. All the bad stuff she wanted me to stop.

But I didn't run straight off.

I stayed here, slumped against the wall.

For hours. Just dreaming of Becky.

I look at Ruby. And feel the guilt again.

She looks back. And for a moment I think she's clapped what I'm feeling. But it's not that. It's the other thing. Wanting what I got. What I'm picking up. I look back at her, listen, wait.

Feel.

'Still not right, Ruby.'

She's thinking the same, Bigeyes. Check her face. She knows something's wrong. But I'll tell you something. She's going to take us in.

Don't ask me how I know.

'Let's go,' she murmurs.

See?

In through the gate.

Bex isn't in the garden.

Stop, check round.

Poky little space, no grass, just concrete slabs piled high with cardboard boxes Ruby's never got round to shunting. Becky's bike propped up in the corner, covered with a piece of canvas and tied under the frame to keep it there.

Even from here I can see it's rusting underneath.

Check out the house. No sounds from inside. Nearest window's the kitchen. I bung a glance at it. No sign of anybody inside. Eyeshine up the wall to the top window. Glint into the landing but nothing more.

Not Bex anyway.

Ruby pulls up the brick behind the bin, checks underneath.

'Key's gone,' she says.

Straightens up, fixes me. I know the look now.

'She's not in there, Ruby.'

'How do you know?'

'I just do.'

'So who's in the house if she's not?'

'Don't know.'

She goes on watching me. I feel Spiky shift close by, and the two dronks. Seth flexes his muscles again. Ruby snaps a glance at him.

'Stay here with Blade,' she tells him. 'Keep your eyes open. If there's trouble, get him away.' Fixes the others. 'You three come with me.'

And before I can say anything, she unlocks the back door and cuts into the house. Spiky's straight after her, followed by the two dronks. I start forward. Can't help it, Bigeyes. I know Bex isn't in there. Might be nobody in there.

But there might be scum waiting.

And it's not right Ruby and the others should take it alone.

But now everything changes. Seth picks it up at the same time. Not from the road but the way we just came, down the alleyway.

Footsteps.

Running towards us.

'Come on,' says Seth.

'We got to warn the others.'

'No time. Got to get you away.'

He pulls me back towards the gate. I chuck a look at the house. Back door's closed and no sign of Ruby and the others crashing back out. They won't have heard what we've heard. But maybe that's as well. They got to stay trimmed on what's in there.

'Come on, boy!' says Seth.

He's yanking me out of the gate now, into the alleyway. Sound of feet's getting louder but no sign yet of who's coming. Only one way to go and that's to the street. We hare down the alleyway, Ruby's house on our left, and still I'm glancing at it, even as I run. I'm desperate for a glimpse of what's going on inside.

But there's no one to be seen.

From behind us comes a shout.

'There!'

I don't look back and neither does Seth. We pile down the alleyway, burst into the street and—shit! Car ploughing in from the left, van from the right. But they're not grinks.

They're porkers.

No sirens, just a scream of brakes, then doors opening, feet slamming the pavement. Seth's got a hand round my arm and he's rushing me away down the road. But it's no good.

I'm slow and he's worse.

Footsteps grow louder. They're closing in fast. Seth goes down. Someone's tackled him from behind. I feel arms lock round me, hoist me off the ground. I kick out but it makes no difference. Guy's too strong and there's another porker ripping in to help him.

Seth's on his feet again, fighting like a bear, but there's three gobbos pinning him back against the wall, heavy bastards, and they know what they're doing.

'Ease off, big man,' says one. 'It's not you we want.'

He takes no notice, struggles to break free. They snag his arms up his back, kick his legs away, drop him to his knees. I call out as the other two bundle me off.

'Leave it, Seth. Nothing you can do.'

He still goes on fighting.

'Seth, leave it, mate.'

I don't see what happens to him. Or what's happening with Ruby in the house. It's fizzing too quick, Bigeyes. I'm over the gobbo's shoulder, bouncing as he carries me to the van. I feel the air spinning, the world spinning with it.

And somewhere in the middle, a picture of Becky.

Perfectly still.

But then it's gone. I'm tumbling into the back of the van, the porker climbing in after me. There's a click of cuffs, a roar of the engine, and we're tearing off down the street.

11

RIGHT AT THE junction, down to the crossing, left past the school. I keep my head down, tracking the streets in my mind. One thing's bung-clear. We're not heading for the nearest police station.

I check the porkers.

Only two, both gobbos. Guy next to me's staring down at the floor of the van. Other gobbo's at the wheel, eyes on the road. I look up at the mirror. No sign of him watching me.

Neither talking.

Flick a glance at the cuffs. Gobbo got 'em on me pretty cute. I'll give him that. My right hand, his left. Frisked me good too. Quick and smart. I think of Poppa. It's what he wanted, I guess. Me going with the porkers. And I was going to give myself up anyway, straight after sorting Bex.

So why doesn't this feel right?

Why don't these gobbos feel right?

I'm thinking, Bigeyes, specially now we're heading away from the next nearest police station. I'm thinking about that business with Bex. Like they knew I was coming. Or loaded the stakes so high in their favour it was worth a punt sending the motors.

Case I turned up.

Like I did.

Something's wrong, Bigeyes.

They're porkers, these guys. No messing. I always know. I've seen too many. And this is a porker van. But what kind of porkers are they? Something feels wrong, Bigeyes. I'm telling you.

We've changed direction again. Not even heading towards the centre of the Beast. Driver's taking us down the east side. We're still north of Mother Grime and cracking in fast, but I got a feeling we're not crossing over.

Told you.

Cutting left, down the underpass, up the other side, left again.

There's no police station down this way, Bigeyes. Not unless the driver's lost. Which he's not. And another thing. No messages getting sent to HQ. Not from these gobbos. Not official messages anyway. They're sitting quiet, like they've been told to say nothing, just do the business.

Yeah, the business.

But what kind of business?

I'm starting to guess the answer.

Right at the lights, over the roundabout, left down the lane towards the warehouses. I've been round here before,

Bigeyes, and I got a bad feeling. Picture of Becky floats into my head again.

And floats out just as quick.

Cos we've stopped.

Driver trigs round the back, opens the door. I clamber out, best I can with the cuff plucking at the other guy's hand. He climbs out with me and now we're walking, over a courtyard, high walls all around, warehouses beyond 'em.

'Funny-looking police station,' I chirp.

They don't answer. We're heading for a gate in the wall, through it, left down a little path, round the back of a building. It's not a warehouse. It's an old office block. In through a side door, down a corridor. Nobody else here.

But the place isn't empty.

I'm telling you, Bigeyes. It's not empty.

Through a door, down another corridor. More narrow than the last. Gobbo with the cuff goes ahead, pulling me after him. Driver tramps behind. I think of the other porkers, the ones wrestling with Seth.

Didn't hear 'em motor after us.

And I'm getting the reason why.

They were just there for the muscle. To make sure of the catch. These two are the delivery boys. And now it's time. To see who wants me.

Door opens and there's the room.

A small, windowless office. Grey, sparse. Filing cabinet in the corner, coat stand next to it. Second door over to the right and just up from that a desk with a gobbo behind it. A senior police officer from his uniform.

Very senior.

But I already know who this is. The face tells me everything. You couldn't miss the resemblance if you tried. But I'd worked out who it was before I got here.

Bex's father.

'Jakes,' I murmur.

He stiffens slightly, bridles even, then gives a smile, leans back in his chair, purrs at me.

'I generally insist on people using my full title. Out of respect for the high office I have the honour to hold.'

He flicks an eye up at the two porkers, then back at me.

'And if that respect is not forthcoming, then I instruct others to do whatever is necessary to produce it.'

I don't answer. I'm still skimming his face. So like Bex's in one way. But nothing like it in others. I think of what she told me. About what he did to her. What he's maybe still doing to her.

But even without knowing that I'd take this guy for slime.

He's still watching me close. I got a feeling he's waiting. For that respect he's just threatened to beat out of me. He glances up at the porkers, pauses. I brace myself. Jakes catches my eye and I feel him smile again.

But it's a hidden smile this time. Just under the eyes.

He looks at the porkers again.

Nods.

I brace myself a second time.

But nothing smashes into my face. Instead the porker with the cuffs tugs me over to the wall by the desk, jerks my arm down, uncuffs his own hand, clips the bracelet onto the radiator, stands back.

And hands Jakes the key.

Jakes pulls open a drawer, drops the key inside, leaves the drawer open.

Gives a flick of his head.

The two porkers trig out of the room, the way we came in. I hear their steps crunching down the corridor, fading, fading. A few moments later, the sound of the van revving up, driving off.

Silence.

Just me standing here, chained to the radiator, and Jakes sitting behind the desk. Watching. Then he reaches into the drawer again. Pulls out a hammer.

I stiffen. Can't help it. Been trying not to flinch but I can't stop it. He catches my fear, smirks, stands up, hammer in his right hand. Walks round to me, stops close by, sits on the edge of the desk.

Easy reach.

Nothing I can do, Bigeyes. They set this up too well. I got my right hand locked and no room to use my left. And that's weak anyway. I take a breath, deep, hard. I got to face up to this dreg.

Whatever he does to me.

He's seen my fear once.

He mustn't see it again.

I twist round, face him best I can. Get ready to spit, snarl, whatever.

He speaks.

'I've been curious to meet you for some time. After all I've heard. And the things Rebecca told me.'

'She told me a few things about you too.'

'She's a little unstable, you know.'

'What have you done to her?'

He looks amused by this.

'How can I do anything to her,' he says, 'when I don't know where she is?'

Shit, Bigeyes. So she really did run away. If this bastard's telling the truth. And then suddenly I clap it. What I kind of suspected all along.

'You sent that text,' I murmur. 'To Ruby. Made out it was from Bex.'

He looks amused again. And I know straightaway I'm right.

'You got everything you needed to know from Bex,' I say. 'Don't tell me how. She ran away again. And you thought if you texted Ruby, I might just show up with her at the house. If you made Bex sound desperate enough.'

He looks down at the hammer, plays with it.

Chuckles.

I try to think. Got to be something I can throw at this slug.

'I've been in touch with Inspector Bannerman,' I start.

'Ah, yes,' he goes. 'Inspector Bannerman. As he was once known.'

'What's that supposed to mean?'

Jakes taps the hammer on the side of the desk, chuckles again.

'I'm afraid you won't find him an Inspector Bannerman any more. Such a sad end to a promising career but you know, alcohol dependence does terrible things. Distorts a man's judgement. It was only a matter of time before he did something disastrous. I gave him all the slack I could, but the last two blunders were just too serious to be overlooked.'

'What are you talking about?'

'Allowing a fourteen-year-old multiple murderer to spend time alone with a three-year-old girl who has already been traumatized by a kidnap. That's bad enough. But then allowing that same murderer to walk away free afterwards, with two knives in his coat pockets. I think you'd have to agree that those are pretty catastrophic errors of judgement.'

I don't answer. I can't think.

Bannerman's finished. That's clear. Probably Fern too. But there was all the stuff I gave him. The information. And the backup drive. Hawk's external hard drive.

I see Jakes watching me. With that hidden smile again.

'Yes,' he murmurs. 'The information was very useful. Very useful indeed.'

And he turns, reaches back into the drawer, pulls something out. Drops it on the desk beside him. I recognize it right away. Haven't seen it for three years.

But it's like I buried it yesterday.

The backup drive from Hawk's computer.

Jakes stands up, smiles down at me. Then stretches up with the hammer and slams it back down again.

Into the drive.

It shatters in one go, pieces flying everywhere, but he goes on beating down with the hammer, a mad grin ripping over his face. Till there's nothing left of the drive.

Or my hopes.

He calms down, stands over me again, raises the hammer once more. I feel myself flinch, in spite of my efforts. He watches me, and a glare of satisfaction darkens his eyes.

Then without another word, he flings the hammer away and strides out of the room. For a few moments I hear his feet pounding the corridor, just like the other two porkers. Then the sound fades. I hear a motor start up, drive off. And silence falls again.

But not for long.

From the door behind comes a click. I twist round, stare towards it. It opens slow. And there's four gobbos standing there.

12

DARKNESS. A COLD stone floor. And me lying on it. Can't see much more. But I know enough. I know I've been knocked out and drugged. I know I've been driven somewhere. I know who's got me. So I know it's the end.

Yeah, Bigeyes.

I won't come back from this.

I got pain slamming my head where they blammed me. Drowsy too but not much, cos they only drugged me a little. They want me awake, Bigeyes. Shit, they want me awake. If you haven't worked out why, you soon will.

Footsteps.

Bang, bang, bang.

I struggle up. Got to be standing. Got to look like I got some spit. Even if I haven't. Crunch of the door, flick of a switch. Light blasts into my face. Single light, straight above me.

I check round quick. Small room, no windows. Long table down the middle, chair close by. Brick walls, nothing on 'em but a blank screen at the far end. Four gobbos in the doorway.

The grinks who came to fetch me from Jakes. They don't waste time. Door clunks closed and they're on me straightaway. Nothing I can do. Except go inside myself. I can't beat 'em, can't escape.

They laugh, pick me up like I'm a doll, dump me on the chair, crowd round, leering. Big gobbos, beefbags, the worst kind of shit. I know what this is, Bigeyes. Oh, yeah. This is trophy time. And here's the man who's won. Right in front of the chair. Face in the screen.

Hawk.

Come to watch the fun.

And celebrate his triumph.

He's sitting in a small room. Somewhere cosy, somewhere far away. Nice easy chair. He's got a casual shirt on, loose at the neck, and his hair's glossy, like it's just been washed. He sips a drink, pops an olive in his mouth. Sees my eye catch him.

Grins.

They push me off the chair, kick me over to the screen, haul me up, stuff my face against the glass. Inches away I see Hawk laughing. He sips his drink again, spears another olive. The gobbos yank me higher.

And there's his eyes, digging into mine like darts. He's going to speak in a moment, going to drip some gloaty words over me. But he doesn't. Just goes on laughing as they pull me away, dump me back on the chair.

I glare back at the face in the screen. I want to drop my head, screw my eyes closed, but I want to glare back too. I want to throw all the hate I got inside me for that smirking bastard. So I make myself glare back, glare back, glare back.

Till I see nothing more.

Cos everything's gone dark.

When I come to, I'm lying on the floor again. I'm aching, shivering. Feel like I've been lying here some time. Don't know for sure. Can't remember what happened at the end. And I don't want to. I just know it's dark and I'm cold.

And it's not over. Oh, no. Bullet in the head? I wish. But it's not going to be like that. Hawk'll want much more than that before he kills me.

Yeah, Bigeyes. I said *he*.

This is personal. He'll let his grinks do the business, and he'll watch every moment, savour every second from his comfy chair. But the final bit. The kill.

He'll do that himself.

Don't ask me how I know.

I try to sit up. Hard to move. I'm aching all over, pain pounding. I keep breaking into tears. I stare about me. Same room. They haven't moved me. They've turned off the light again but I can see enough now.

Table, chair, screen—blank again, thank Christ.

And me, whimpering.

I make myself stand up. Floor's slippery with blood. Got to be mine. They must have knocked me about a bit at the end. I don't remember. Just remember the darkness. I reach up, feel my face.

Sticky round the nose and mouth.

I step over the blood, plod to the far corner of the room. Darker there and I want darkness right now. I slump down, huddle back against the wall, pull my knees into my chest.

Feel the tears come back.

I'm so scared, Bigeyes. Scared of death and even more scared of torture. And both those things are coming. Trust me. I know how this works. First the gloating. So I know he's got me. Then the wait. An hour, two hours, whatever. To make my mind do what it's doing now.

Spin pictures of what's going to happen.

And then they'll come back. And it'll start.

Hawk's won. He's got everything he wanted. Jakes working for him as his personal poodle. The computer backup drive destroyed. The gangster bojos'll give him some sludge, but they won't have enough to plug him.

Not on their own. It needed the porkers to do their bit, and now Bannerman's finished, that's over too. Specially with Jakes in charge. Like I say, Hawk's got everything. And now he's got me too. And he'll be loving that.

He'll squeeze my life out slow as he can.

And lick all the juice as it goes.

Then I hear it.

Click of the door. It's opening again and I can see a figure standing there. For a moment I think it's Hawk. But it's too early for that. He won't come for me till I'm right at the end. Too weak to move, too weak to beg.

This is someone else.

Just a shadow so far. Gobbo, yeah, but still a shadow. He's just standing there, peering in. Searching the darkness, for me surely. Maybe he can't see me yet. I keep still, try to think.

There's something familiar about this guy.

But I can't crack what it is.

And there's something else.

He's wary. He's looking for me, yeah, no question. Who else would he be looking for? But he's standing there on the edge, and he's got the door half-open. I'm sensing he's on his own. And I got a feeling he's not supposed to be here.

So it's private.

Whatever this is.

Now I got him. I recognize the shape. The neck, the head. He was in the car, Bigeyes. At the school, yeah? He was one of the minders looking after Damien. Not the driver. The other grink.

And now I'm guessing the rest.

I rammed their motor, remember? And the last thing I saw of those two was this gobbo chasing after me. And his mate slumped over the steering wheel. I might just have killed him. Which case this gobbo's here for some justice.

On behalf of his mate.

That could be bad.

But it might also be good. It might even be a chance. Cos I'm telling you, Bigeyes, whatever this guy's come for, he'll know he can't kill me. It'd be more than his slimy life's worth if he deprives Hawk of his kill. And he won't forget that for a second.

So he's taking a risk here. And he's got to watch his step.

Like I got to watch mine.

He's coming in. Seen me now, worked out where I am, safe in the corner. No chance of escape. He closes the door, locks it on the inside. Drops the key in his right pocket. I keep still, check him cute as I can.

Hard to tell if he's got a knife. He won't use one anyway. Too dangerous for him. Cos even if it doesn't kill me, it'll leave a mark. He'll use fists and feet. And hope the blood and bruises get mixed up with the rest.

He's walking over.

Slow.

13

I SCRAMBLE UP, struggle towards the chair. Only weapon in the room. But he cuts me off easy. Stands there, blocking my way, glowering. He's not here for fun, this gobbo. Not leering like Hawk. Or just carrying out orders like the four grinks.

This one's raging. And I know I'm right. It's for his mate. He doesn't talk. Just comes for me.

Fast, low.

Plunges into me, rams me against the wall, flings me on the ground, falls on me. I feel my breath rasp out, and now I'm choking. He's got his hands tight round my throat and he's squeezing, squeezing.

I stare up into his face. His eyes are black blades and he's got spittle round his mouth. He tightens his grip. Jesus, Bigeyes. He's going for it. He's not going to hold back like I thought. He's saying stuff you, Hawk, I'm stiffing this bastard for myself.

Then I feel it, thank Christ. A hesitation in his hands, just a flash, like he's suddenly remembered. I stretch out, crunch his groin in my fist. He gives a roar, slams my hand away, yanks me to my feet, butts me in the face.

I stagger, head swimming. He grabs me by the collar, hurls me towards the other side of the room. I thump onto the floor, skid past the table, smack the chair on its side. Squirm back up, quick as I can, but I'm stunned, I'm struggling to see.

Gobbo's lumbering over.

I snap hold of the chair, whip it round in front of me. Won't do much good but it's all I got. Gobbo takes no notice of it, comes on. He's spitting hate now and he won't hold back again.

He breaks into a run, like he can't wait. I brace myself. He dips his shoulder, charges, skids on the patch of blood. Stays upright but he's off balance and I won't get a better chance. I step to the side, swing the chair, smash his legs away.

He falls against the side of the table, grasps hold of it, half-standing. I crash the chair over his head. He gives a moan, tumbles to the ground. I slam the chair over him again. He rolls away, lurches back up.

Turns to face me again.

I grip the chair, edge round, keeping the table between us. He's got blood pouring from his mouth and nose, but his eyes are darker than ever. He seizes the table, jerks it out of the way, blunders towards me.

Then stops, swaying on his feet.

I stare at him. His eyes are misting up. So are mine but his are worse. I twist the chair, hold it so the legs are pointing at him, charge. None of 'em catch his face but they lock round it, cage him in, and now I'm driving him back, back, back.

Smash!

The glass screen shatters as his head plunges into it. He gives a bellow, flails his arms. His body's heaving and rolling under me, but I go on driving him back, into the screen, into the broken glass.

Then stop.

Stand back, wait.

Chair poised.

The gobbo writhes, groans. His head's stuck in the broken screen, shattered glass sprinkling his hair. He shudders, pulls himself clear, moaning as the shards rip into him. His eyes are drowning but he fixes me with 'em.

I grip the chair, aim, lunge.

He goes down.

And this time doesn't come up.

I stand over him, panting. He's not dead. He's still breathing, but he's out cold. I got to be quick. No telling how long he'll stay out. And the other grinks could turn up any moment.

I drop to my knees, run through his pockets.

Key to the door, mobile, fob for his car.

Stuff everything in my pocket, stand up, take a breath. I'm swaying bad and my head's like a fog. Body's hurting worse than ever and I got blood slopping off me again. Some of it's this bastard's.

He stirs, just a bit. I step back, check him. He's still again, but I got a feeling he's picking up. I limp over to the door, put my ear to it. No sounds outside. Got to risk it. Key in, turn, ease the door ajar.

Listen again.

Still nothing.

Check through the gap. Dark corridor, no lights, no figures. Bung a glance back in the room. Gobbo's still lying there, not moving. Step out into the corridor, close the door, lock it, check round.

Same as before. Silence, darkness, nobody in sight.

Corridor goes only one way. Set off down it, shuffling with the pain. Can't run. If they come for me, I'm dead. No way I can run. Not now. Been hurt too bad. I can hardly stand. Vision's going and I'm bumbling like a duff.

Don't let me lose it, Bigeyes.

If I keel over, I'm grilled. I got to stay upright, got to keep walking. And stay alert somehow. Cos Christ knows where I am and how many grinks I got to wig it from.

End of the corridor. It's turning left. Stop, check round the corner.

Another corridor, but it's short, and there's a small door at the end. Down to it, panting like before, stop. Jesus, Bigeyes, don't let it be locked. Please don't let it be locked. Cos I can see straight off my key won't fit.

Shit, it's locked. And I can't pick this one. Wrong kind.

I lean against the door, gasping for breath, head spinning worse than ever. I try to think. I was sure I got everything out of that grink's pockets. But he wouldn't have slammed his way into this building if he couldn't get out again. So he must have brought a key for this door.

And either he hid it somewhere in the corridor to make double sure I can't get out. Or he's got it in another pocket and I missed it. So I got to go looking. Nothing else for it.

Cos there's no other way out. No window anywhere to crawl through. And no other door but this one. Hawk chose a good place for his filthy work. I start off down the corridor—then catch a sound.

Footsteps.

Scramble back to the door, put an ear to it.

Silence again. But I'm sure I heard something. For a moment I feel a chill of panic, like that gobbo's broken out of the room and he's coming for me. Then I catch the sound again, and it's steps, and they're not coming from down the corridor.

But from the other side of this door.

And they're heading towards it.

I dive to the side, just in time. Rattle of a key in the lock, then the door swings open. I crouch behind it, low as I can, fists clenched. All I got left now. Fists. Cos whoever's coming in's going to clap me the moment they turn to close the door.

And if it's more than one grink, I got no chance at all.

Got no chance anyway, even with one.

Door swings into me and there's a tramp of feet through the gap. Door starts to swing closed again. I get ready to fight.

But the tramping feet go on.

I crouch there, staring. It's the four grinks who worked me over before and they're striding down the corridor, none looking back. The last gobbo simply left the door to shut by itself.

It's already nearly closed.

I reach out, catch it before it locks, check the gobbos again. They're turning into the long corridor but still in sight. I hold my breath, wait . . .

They disappear from view.

And I'm out the door.

14

CHECK ROUND, QUICK, quick. They'll be out again any second, moment they see what's happened. And I'm getting groggier with every step. Blink round. Hard to see where I am. Darkness is falling and there's a storm blowing up.

Lane straight ahead, walls either side. Think it bends off to the right. Got to hit that point and get round it before the grinks burst out. Nowhere else to go. I blunder off, best I can. Head's clouding and I'm hurting like I want to scream.

Bend in the lane. Least I got this far. Check back. Place I was in looks like some kind of outhouse. No other buildings nearby. But I got no time to think of that. I'm desperate to find that grink's car. Just praying it's somewhere close, somewhere on its own.

But I don't suppose there's much chance of that.

I stumble on, up the next part of the lane. Dirt track running off it to another outhouse, up on the rise. Van and three cars parked outside. I hobble towards 'em. Got to go for it, Bigeyes, got to take a risk. I stagger on, up the slope, up the slope, fast as I can go.

But it's horribly slow.

Storm's getting stronger and the wind's loud up here on the higher ground. But I still catch the slam of the door behind me, and the sound of footsteps charging after me. I limp on, closer, closer. Here's the second outhouse. Here are the motors. I stab the key fob at 'em. Car on the left flashes, unlocks.

Check behind.

No sign of the grinks yet but they won't be long. From inside the outhouse comes the sound of gobbos laughing. Jesus, Bigeyes. Don't let 'em rip out now. Open the car door, soft as I can, jump in, key in the ignition, check round.

Got to be something, got to be something. Rummage in the glove compartment—nothing. Lockers, doors, tray under the steering column—nothing. Under the driver's seat—gotcha.

Screwdriver.

I was hoping for a knife but this'll do.

Out of the car and now there's figures racing up the track. Same four grinks and they're bawling into the storm to their mates in the outhouse. I crash over to the van, plunge the screwdriver into the front tyre, over to the other motors, same again.

Back to the car, jump in, flick on the central locking.

Start the engine.

Figures swarming round now. The gobbos from the track and more grinks pouring out of the outhouse. Two jump on the bonnet, two more on the roof. I rev up, ease the clutch. The car brays and thunders forward.

Rain's pelting down now, hard, heavy drops, but still there's gobbos piling onto the car. Three on the bonnet, four, five. More throwing 'emselves on the roof. Car's moving but groaning under the weight.

I swerve, swerve again. Grinks tip off both sides. But some are still clinging on. I spin the wheel, left, right. More bodies fly off. Nobody left on the bonnet now. Don't know about the roof.

Check the mirror. Figures behind me, rolling on the ground. Hard to tell if I got 'em all off the car. But I think so.

Thump!

A fist smacks into the side window. Glass doesn't shatter, but the fist tries again. I see the guy's face upside down, fuming in at me from the top of the car. Christ knows how he's hanging on. I speed up, race for the end of the track.

Slam the brake.

Car skids to a halt. A dark form torpedoes off the roof, bounces on the bonnet, rolls over the ground in front of the car. Gives a shudder, starts to stand up. But I'm moving again, foot down, speeding up, speeding up.

Gobbo turns, glowers at me.

'Yeah, grink,' I murmur. 'Stay there if you want.'

He jumps aside at the last minute.

And I scream past.

Down the lane, searching hard. I didn't see a way out before. Just the track heading up to the second outhouse. There's got to be another way out of wherever this is. Cos I'm telling you, Bigeyes. I got no idea where we are.

Snap on the headlights, full beam.

There's the first outhouse, where they kept me. And now I can see better. This lane bends round the building and off past it. Christ knows where it goes after that but I got no choice. Can't go back.

Bump past the outhouse, on down the lane. It's twisting and falling, dronky broken walls either side. No clue where this ends up. Just got to hope it takes us to a main road. And then we got to pelt.

Cos I'll tell you something, Bigeyes. This area's going to be flooded in minutes. Never mind me stuffing the tyres back there. That'll help but only a bit. There'll be backup cracking in here before you can blink.

If I don't break out in ten minutes, I won't break out at all.

Lane's still falling. Hilly little place, whatever this is. Don't recognize any of it. Touch of the country but not leafy green. Hard to see with the darkness and rain. And my head's not helping.

Eyes are blearing up again.

And my body's blamming.

I forgot about both in the gig back there, but now I'm loose, it's all come back. I got to grip hard, keep my spit, or I'll crash this motor right now. Shake my head, shake it again, peer out.

Wipers. Use the bloody wipers. See, Bigeyes? I'm not thinking right. Should have stuck 'em on first go. Feel round, find the wiper switch, flick 'em on.

Junction straight ahead.

Stop, check for a signpost.

Nothing.

Left, off down the road. Don't ask me why I turned this way. Got no idea. Foot down, squeal the motor. Least this baby can shift. Keep my eyes on the road and the lights digging through the cloud of rain. It's growing heavier all the time. Trees on both sides of the road now, bending with the wind.

Another junction. No sign like before.

Left again.

Just a hunch.

Or not even that. Just got to keep moving. Keep moving and hope.

Foot down again. Headlights coming the other way. I check 'em close. Could be anything. It's a lorry. I watch it cute, but it's straight past. More headlights, opposite side.

I keep going, keep watching. They all pass. I drive on, fast, fast. Hoping for another junction. I want to get off this road now. Been on it too long. And I want a signpost. I want to know where those bastards took me.

Garage on the left, police car by one of the pumps. No sign of anyone filling up. But there's two porkers in the station, talking to the girl on duty. I flash past. Check the mirror.

No one coming after me.

Drive on, faster still. Got to put all the distance I can between me and anyone else. And the road's clear for the moment so I'm hoping the speed won't attract attention. But I need another junction. I need it soon.

Roundabout, big one. And a huge great signboard to go with it.

OK, OK.

I got where we are now. They took me north of the Beast, Bigeyes. Right out to where the green country starts. Cute little place for a torture chamber, right? And Hawk'll have plenty more like that.

You better believe it.

Onto the roundabout, last exit, off down the road.

Yeah, Bigeyes, I know.

You're wondering why I'm heading back towards the Beast. You're thinking—you got away from the grinks and you got a nice fast car. So why not use it? Why not drive north, far as you can. Petrol gauge says full tank so why not use up all the juice, dump the motor, wig it further, go to ground? You might just live.

Yeah, Bigeyes. I might just live.

Only it won't work now. That kind of living. Cos there's something I've found out since I met Becky, and Mary, and Jaz, and Ruby, and Poppa, and even a few others. Like Bex and Bannerman.

I've found out there's things you can't ever run away from. Cos they just keep running with you. If you don't know what I'm talking about, tough. Cos I'm not explaining it. I just know I'm not running. I'm going back.

Cos there's one last thing to do.

15

IF I CAN stay alive long enough. That's the smack-end of it. And I don't just mean grinks rubbing me out. I mean my body giving up. Cos I can feel my life dribbling out by itself.

They hurt me bad, those bastards. I'm struggling to see, struggling to stay upright. I want to slop over, close my eyes, fade away, not come back. But I can't let that happen. Not yet. Got to do this last thing.

It's sitting there in my head, fighting the darkness that's already there. But I can still see it, this thing. Cos it's got a darkness of its own. A bigger darkness. I just hope I can live long enough to slam it through. Only . . .

Shit!

Car's swerving off the road. Jerk the wheel, swing us back on course, check the mirror, breathe out. Breathe again. Bloody hell, Bigeyes. I lost it, lost focus. Still losing focus. See what I mean?

My eyes are fogging up again.

Got to pull over, rest, just a bit, get my head right. I need a lay-by, or better still, a quiet road, somewhere dark. No sign of anywhere yet, and the traffic's building up too. Both ways, specially coming up behind, heading for the Beast.

Christ!

I'm swerving again.

Blare of a horn behind me. I pull the car straight, hide my face, feel a car scream past. Another blare of the horn as it goes. Look back at the road. Jesus, Bigeyes, this is bad.

I got to rest. And soon.

Lay-by, just ahead. Don't like the look of it. Too exposed. But I got no choice. Another minute on the road and I'll crash. Slow down, easy, easy. Got to look like everything's cute. No waggling the car.

Indicate, brake, pull in. Take a breath, think. Handbrake up. Good boy. Lights off, wipers off. Kill the engine. Breathe.

Traffic roars past, thundering towards the Beast. I can't stay long, Bigeyes. Too risky. Any neb can see me parked here and grinks'll be ploughing up this road. Porkers too.

Just a couple of minutes. No more.

Can't sleep. Mustn't sleep.

Close my eyes.

Mustn't sleep.

But it falls over me like a shroud. A big, black shroud, deep and warm and good—till the nightmare starts.

And Christ, I'm back in that room. I didn't get away, and Hawk's still watching me, grinning, grinning. And it's not just him now but other nebs too. It's like a gallery of faces, each one in its own little glass screen. They're all round the room, staring out.

And it's not just grinks. It's people who shouldn't be watching. It's Becky and Jaz and Mary. And now other faces. Bannerman and Fern. Ruby, Poppa and all their mates. Trixi and the trolls. Dig and Riff. And more faces, nebs from the past. The people I killed.

And suddenly I get it, Bigeyes.

Everyone's watching. That's right. Everyone I've ever known, good or bad. They're all watching. I'm in the room and I can't get away and the grinks are starting to rip up my life, one piece at a time.

'Ah!'

I'm awake. I'm gripping the steering wheel, my body shaking, my head blasting like it wants to split open. I lean back, gaping with the pain. And catch a glint of headlights in the mirror.

Someone's pulling in to the lay-by.

I try to calm down, get my head straight. Don't know who this is but I'm not waiting to find out. Start the engine, lights on, check mirror, pull out. Check mirror again. Other motor's stopped in the lay-by. Gobbo in a suit, naffing into a mobile.

Nobody with him.

But he's staring in my direction.

Might mean nothing. Speed up, check the mirror again. Other car's pulled out too, coming on fast but staying in my wake. Gobbo's still talking into his mobile. Catches me up, snaps in behind, puts his mobile down.

I go on watching him. He stays there for a bit, then starts to pull out. I whip my face the other way as he roars past. Check after him. He's blasting on now but I go on watching him till he disappears among the lights ahead.

I'm doing this all wrong, Bigeyes. Just shows I got my brain smashed. I never should have come this way. Too busy. That gobbo might be nothing, just some fancy dimp showing off his motor.

But I'm too big a target on this road.

Should have snagged off way back. Trouble is, I'm so weak and that's what fixed me on this road. I've only got so much spit left in me so I thought I better take the fastest route.

But maybe I'm zipping myself over. Cos if I'm honest with you, Bigeyes, I wasn't really thinking about the fastest route. Truth is—I just wasn't thinking. About anything.

So I better start now.

OK, got to wig it off this road. That's the first thing. Take the straggly way into the Beast. Never mind how weak I'm feeling. Got to take the safest route. Won't be much better than this road, but it might be a bit.

Rain's stopped. Wind's gone down.

Junction ahead.

I watch it, cute as I can. Cuts off round the north of the Beast, but there's roads off it I can use. Side roads, little

lanes. Going to take a while to get in. But I got to crack
that. However much I'm hurting.

Left, off the road.

Down to the roundabout, second exit, right at the motel,
over the bridge, past the shops. Check the car clock. Six in the
evening. Jesus, Bigeyes. Was I that long with those bastards? I
lost all track of time. And now the night's coming back.

Switch on the radio. Got to hear this one.

'The news at six o'clock.'

And I feel my mouth drop open. Cos I'm the first item.
It's all about me. My name, my life, stuff they've pieced
together. The number of dronks I killed. How I ran away to
the old city, played dead, made friends with Mary, ran off
with Bex and Jaz. Came back to the Beast. How I'm dangerous, how I'm still at large. How I shouldn't be approached.

It's all in the bulletin.

Except one thing.

Lord Haffler-Devereaux.

No mention of him at all. Just stuff about me getting
mixed up in the gangster underworld. But what did you
expect? Jakes will have cherry-picked the bits he wanted
from Bannerman's report.

The news goes on.

More violence, more arrests in the Beast. Only telling
us so much. No names, like before. But I'm thinking
names, Bigeyes. You bet. Names from the past, names I
wrote down on those lists. Not just the bojos and gangster
dregs but the city nebs, bankers, business bums and other
spikes from Hawk's smoky world.

And the biggest name of all.

Lord Haffler-Devereaux.

I wish those names were on the news. Christ, I do.

The bulletin goes bumbling on. But I'm only half-listening now. I got the drift. The net's spreading wider and that's good. Yeah, Bigeyes, that's very good. Only problem is, it's nowhere near good enough.

Not to nail Hawk.

The gangster bojos won't get him on their own. Nor will the porkers. He'll stay safe from all the grime and sweep away every track that leads to him. He can sit cute in his nest, specially now he knows the backup drive from his computer's been slammed.

He'll be mad though. I'm telling you, Bigeyes. He might be safe but his world's crumbling around him and he'll be out of his mind with rage. And that's what I'm counting on. I need him to be mad.

For what I got planned.

16

OK, THINK. STAY awake, stay alive, and think.

Radio off, check the road. Two things I got to do quick and there's a place just round the corner that's cute for both. Long as it's not too crowded. And the payphone's still working.

Cos I don't want to use the grink's mobile. Not for this. Don't want him tracing the number I rang. Good news is I spotted something in the glove compartment earlier when I was looking for a blade to stab the tyres. Something I'm hoping I can use.

I'll show you later.

On down the road, round the corner.

There you go. Garage, phone box, burger kiosk. And only a few nebs hanging round. Pull in, drive over to the far side of the parking area, check round. No cars nearby. Lights off, engine off.

Check again.

Nobody looking, nobody coming over. Just a few cars parked here. Three nebs by the kiosk, nobody in the phone box. Reach over, open the glove compartment. There it is, Bigeyes.

A wallet.

Nice fat one too, so I'm hoping there's some decent jippy inside. And I'm going to need it. Cos I got to spend some money tonight. Right, let's see what the bastard had on him.

Jesus, this'll help. And all in crispy notes. Won't be enough though. I'm still going to have to crawl back into that tunnel I showed you. Remember it? The old snake-hole where I stashed the money?

Going to need all of that.

And probably still have to barter.

Anyway, let's get on with it.

Stuff the notes in my pocket, poke about the wallet for some loose change. Yeah, plenty. Let's go. And hope our boy's in tonight.

Over to the phone box. Couple of faces check me out from the cars. Couple more from the kiosk. I keep my face dark in the hood. New car drives in, swishes into a parking space.

Flash motor.

Two gobbos in suits. They don't get out. Just sit there, talking.

Looking round.

I step into the phone box, check for a dialling tone. It's cute. Flick a glance round at the car park. Gobbos still sitting in the flash motor. Nobody looking my way. I got to do this. Whatever else is going on.

Coins, number, dial.

He better be in, Bigeyes. He better bloody be in.

Click of the phone. Sound of a television. And a radio. Then a voice.

'Yeah?'

'Hello, Ezi.'

He doesn't answer. I hurry on, before he kills the phone.

'It's Blade.'

'I worked that out.'

'I see Nelson's been busy.'

'Yeah, man. He got one big shopping list.'

'He must be pleased with you.'

'What's your point?'

Slam of a car door. I check the parking area. One of the suits has got out. Trigging over to the kiosk. Other gobbo's staying put. I go on.

'There's something I want you to get me.'

'Like what?'

I take a breath. I'm choked about this, Bigeyes. Choked out of my head. I'm weak and I'm hurt and I'm not thinking good, and I need Ezi to do this badly. He's the only neb I'll ever talk into getting me what I want.

'Like what?' he snaps.

I tell him, slow as I can, clear as I can. What I want, what it's for. He hears me through, then chuckles.

'Sure you want this?'

'Why not?'

'Don't sound like your kind of style, boy.'

'It's what I want,' I say. 'And you got no cause to complain. I told you what I want it for.'

'You sure did.'

'So it's going to end up helping you big time, right?'

'Oh, yeah.' Ezi chuckles again. 'It's gonna help us big time.'

I check the parking area again. Kiosk's almost cleared. The other nebs have gone back to their cars and it's just the gobbo in the suit getting served.

I take a breath. So far, so good.

But now it gets tougher.

'I need it tonight, Ezi.'

'Oh, is that so?' he gloats. 'Man in a hurry, right?'

'Can you do it? And how much will it cost?'

He doesn't chuckle this time. He laughs out loud.

'I can get that for you in two hours. And it ain't gonna cost you nothing. No, sir. Considering what we gonna get when you done finished, you can have that baby for free. With Mr Nelson's blessings on top.'

He laughs again, a long, mocking laugh.

Don't like the way this is going, Bigeyes. I know Ezi can get me what I want and I expected him to chew me up a bit before he agreed. What's bothering me is—will he deliver?

I didn't expect a freebie. I thought I'd have to pay. I almost want to pay. Cos that way I got a chance of him turning up with something. Even if I have to fight him for it. But if he's just having fun, I could get nothing. Or worse still, turn up and get spiked.

But I guess I got no choice.

'OK,' I start, 'I'll meet you at—'

'No, no,' he cuts in. 'You don't tell me where to meet. I tell you. You got that?'

I frown. I knew he'd bomb me on this. I don't like it, Bigeyes. It could be more than him having fun. He might be setting me up for another gig with him and Spit. And this time they'll come prepared.

'I'm not coming to your flat,' I say.

'I don't want you in my flat. You been there once already and I don't want your smell back.' He pauses. 'End of my estate there's a park with a playing field. You know it?'

'Yeah.'

'Bottom of that there's some trees.'

'I know 'em.'

Shit place to meet, Bigeyes. For me anyway. Cute enough for Ezi if he's planning to jump me with Spit and their mates. Cos they got a hundred places to hide among all those shadows.

'Meet me there in two hours,' he says.

And hangs up.

Can't say I'm surprised, Bigeyes. I kind of expected this. Or something like it. But I guess that's how things are now. All or nothing. I step out of the phone box, dip my head further inside the hood, trig over to the kiosk.

Nobody there now, just the gobbo behind the counter. Smell of burgers and onions cooking. I wander up, face low. Gobbo chirps out at me.

'What can I do for you, mate?'

'Two burgers, two lots of chips, two cans of Coke.'

'Onions?'

'Yeah, thanks.'

I catch him bung a look round the car park. Don't know if he saw me turn up on my own in the grink's car. I'm hoping not cos if he did, he'll be wondering about my age.

With any luck he just thinks I'm ordering for two and some other neb's driving the car I came in. But he goes on looking round the car park. I got to stop him doing that.

'Can I have some ketchup with it?'

He looks back at me.

'Some ketchup?' I say. 'Please.'

He sniffs, fixes the food. I half-turn, wait.

'There you go,' he mutters.

I give him the money, take the food, wander off towards the garage. Got to head this way for a bit, make him think I'm nothing to do with that motor at the other end of the car park.

I walk a bit further, check round, cut right, out of his sight-line, trig back behind the kiosk, round it to the car. Stop, check round.

Nobody watching me from the other motors, far as I can tell. And someone else has stepped up to the kiosk and the gobbo behind the counter's turned to fix more food.

Slip into the car, hood down, start up. Drive off, keeping to the edge of the car park. Turn my face away from the kiosk and the other motors. Don't know if anyone's worked me out. But there's nothing I can do about that now.

Back on the road, down to the lights, straight over, left at the junction. Gobbling the burgers as I go. Jesus, they taste good. Two lots? I wish I'd bought three. I didn't just buy two so I could spin that gobbo's head. I bought 'em cos I'm starving.

The chips go the same way as the burgers.

So does the Coke.

Drive on, watching, watching.

Getting close now, Bigeyes. And I'm choking again. I hate this estate. Worried about the time too. Two hours, Ezi said. That would have been no bum gripe if it hadn't been for the gobbo in the kiosk. I wasted precious minutes stinging that dimp.

Round the roundabout, past the cinema, left at the lights.

And there it is, down at the bottom of the hill. Recognize that? Block of flats where Ezi hangs out. Only last time we came, we hit it from the other side. I'm keeping away from that end, Bigeyes.

You know why?

Cos we're not crossing the playing field to get to the trees. That way they can hide and watch me coming. We'll park over there on the right and I'll climb the fence into the trees and come at 'em from the other direction.

That way I might get a chance to check who's there before I show myself.

Just hope I got enough strength to scrape over that fence.

Check round, wait for a gap in the traffic, pull over. Check again. Nobody on the pavement. Engine off, lights off. Wait. Check over the road.

There's the fence, see? And the trees on the other side. You can just get a glimpse of the playing field beyond. Glance at the car clock.

Dead on time.

So they should be there.

Yeah, Bigeyes. It won't just be Ezi.

Out of the car. Don't slam the door. Close it soft. Over the road, quiet, slow. Eyeshine over the fence. Think I can climb that. Hang on, I don't need to. I can squeeze through that gap down there.

Creep over, scrape through.

Grass under my feet and hard bony roots. Stop at the first tree, peer round. No sign of Ezi or anyone else. Just shadowy trunks reaching up to the sky. I take a step forward, another, another. Then hear a voice growl behind me.

'Get the bastard!'

17 I WHIRL ROUND, brace myself—and see Ezi standing there. He's slipped between me and the fence and he's blocking my way back to the street. No sign of him carrying what I came for. But he'll be carrying something.

A gun probably.

I check round me. No sign of any other nebs.

Look back at Ezi.

And see him laughing. He doesn't speak, just goes on mocking, like he did on the phone. I go on checking round. He could still have slugs backing him up. Spit's bound to be here somewhere.

Ezi catches my thought.

'He ain't here, man.'

I check again. Ezi shakes his head.

'Spit ain't here. Nobody ain't here. Just you and me.'

I still don't believe him. And why hasn't he got the stuff I asked for? He catches that thought too.

'It's over there.' He nods into the trees. 'Didn't feel like carrying it to the fence.'

'What did you come over here for anyway?'

'Cos I guessed you'd climb over. Wouldn't risk crossing the field. Too easy to spot. So I thought I'd give you a surprise.'

Ezi starts laughing again.

'You see? Not that clever, are you?'

He stops suddenly, fixes me.

'You're hurt, man.'

I shrug.

'Let's get on with it.'

He takes no notice, steps over, peers into my face.

'You hurt bad. Who done that?'

I don't answer. Ezi goes on staring at me. And there's something in his face, Bigeyes. Something I'd never have expected. Not friendship. Jesus, no. But I'll tell you one thing. He's stopped laughing at me.

But I don't like him watching me like this.

'I'm in a hurry, Ezi,' I mutter.

He straightens up, still watching me close.

'Is that so? Well, let's get moving.'

He turns, leads me into the trees, stops just before the playing field opens up.

'There,' he says.

Points to a lumpy bag resting on a stump. Bends down, picks it up.

'You got everything I asked for?' I say.

'See for yourself.'

He holds out the bag. I take it, poke about inside. It's all there. Even the extra bits.

'All ready to go,' says Ezi. He pauses. 'Sure you still want this?'

'Yeah.'

'It's mean shit.'

'Yeah, yeah.'

'I'll show you how it works,' he goes.

He doesn't need to. I can see how it works. But I let him tell me. He runs through it, thorough. Shows me twice. I feel myself fidget. I just want him to go. So I can go. And get this thing done.

'Piece of piss,' I say.

He looks up at me.

'Oh, it ain't hard. Ain't hard at all. Even a kid could handle it. And you ain't no kid.'

I stare back at him. Can't read his voice, Bigeyes. Or his face. Is he mocking me again? And why'm I bothered if he is? I shouldn't give two bells. But I do. For some reason. I hear myself speak. And suddenly I sound so young.

'I'm fourteen, Ezi.'

Why did I say that, Bigeyes? Eh? To this dronk, of all people. It just came out, like I couldn't stop it. There's a silence, a long silence. Ezi looks back at me, quizzical, then gives a slow smile.

'You ain't fourteen,' he says.

Leans close, whispers.

'You's as old as sin, brother.'

And he turns and walks off over the field.

I watch him go. He's trigging slow, steady, taking his time. Doesn't look back once. Weird, Bigeyes. I almost want him to. But he goes on walking, step step step, a moving shadow, getting fainter all the time.

And then he's gone.

I'm shaking again. Pain's banging my head, my body. I open the bag, look inside. Feel the pain go on. Close the bag, clench my fists, turn, limp back to the fence.

Got to do this.

Nothing else left.

Whatever Becky thinks, and Mary, and Jaz, and Ruby, and Poppa, and Christ knows who else. Cos I'm telling you, Bigeyes, they're all shouting no. I can hear 'em right now, among the swaying trees.

No, no, no.

That's what they're saying.

And I'm saying—it's got to be this way.

Through the gap in the fence, back to the street, check round. Traffic moving, both ways. Smellies, taxis, motors. Picking up too. Got to watch myself, specially with this bag. Got to clap everything that moves, before it hits.

Wait for a gap, check faces, over the road, back to the motor. Jump in, check again. Nobody stopping, nobody ripping over. Bag on my lap. Feels strange lumped there. Can't drive like this, but I want it near me.

I know it's a risk, if I get stopped.

But I want it near me. Not in the boot. Push it over the passenger seat, down onto the floor, straighten up again.

Take a breath. Take another. Check the petrol gauge. Still plenty. Enough for what I need anyway.

Whip a glance at the car clock.

Half past eight. Let's go.

Start up, check round, wait for a spot, pull out. Down to the bottom of the road, round the round-about, back the way we came. Yeah, Bigeyes, now you're wondering. Why are we heading north again?

Never mind. I'm too tired to explain. And I got too much to think about. And watch for. The roads are going to be worse now I got away from Hawk. Every grink'll be out, and every porker too. The good porkers and the dodgy ones.

But you know what's strange? I've almost stopped worrying. Don't know why. I should be worrying. I will be later. Before dawn certainly. I'll be choked out of my head by then.

But right now, when there's most eyes watching for me, I'm just cute about driving. Sitting here driving, sweet on the speed limit, nice and legal. Steady steady. Like the way Ezi walked out of my life.

And here's something I hadn't expected. About driving steady. It's good for thinking. I told you just now I got lots to think about. Well, I have. But there's a second strange thing. About driving steady, I mean.

I'm getting a different kind of thinking.

I was going to think about what I got to do.

What's coming up.

But all I can think about is how beautiful the night looks. Yeah, Bigeyes, even here, cracking through the

Beast. The lights of the shops, pubs, houses. The lights of the motors. The black sky reaching over us. And me, here, in this little moving snug. I've almost forgotten it's a grink's motor.

Cos it's not now.

It's mine. My little motor. My little moving snug.

Drive on, north, north, and now we're cutting west. Yeah, Bigeyes, heading right out to the edges of the Beast. Not where those bastards took me for their bit of sport. We're cutting west of that, and slamming further.

Out of the Beast altogether.

On, on, time ticking and my thoughts ticking with it. One hour, two, three, and still on. Check around you, Bigeyes. See how the roads have changed? The Beast has faded away and his energy's faded too. He's still there, heaving behind us, but cop this instead.

Main roads have gone and we're on a country lane. You're wondering how I know my way. Tough. Keep wondering. You should know me by now anyway. How I remember stuff.

Junction at the end. Right at the church, through the village, out the other side. Yeah, Bigeyes. We're not stopping here. We got a bit further to drive. And then a long walk after that.

On, on, climbing now, up the straggly lane. It narrows here. I remember it so well. There you go. Just hope we don't meet someone coming the other way. But we should be cute this time of night. And there's never much moving round here.

Look over at the bag in front of the passenger seat.
First time I've glanced at it since I dumped it there.
Not quite sure why.

I take my eyes off it, check the lane ahead. Still climbing, see? And then it dips off to the right. Top of the hill, stop, handbrake on. Keep the engine running. Lean back in the seat.

I'm breathing fast, Bigeyes. Too fast. But I can't stop myself.

Turn off the engine. Feel the silence fall over me. But I can still hear my breathing. I hate the sound of it. Kind of scares me. Reach out, turn on the radio.

More news. And it's the same again. Violence, arrests. My name in the bulletin. No mention of Lord Haffler-Devereaux. And there won't be. Trust me, Bigeyes.

They won't get him.

Radio off, take a breath. Climb out of the car. Feel the silence again. Funny how the storm died away so quick. Even if there's another one coming soon. I stand there, stare round.

Lane rolls away to the right, falling into the valley below. To the left, a track running down the side of the field, and right at the bottom, a lake glistening in the night, moonlight dancing on the surface.

So beautiful, Bigeyes. And you know what? I've been picturing that lake. No kidding. I remember it so well. I used to dream about it when I was sleeping rough in the old city.

A good memory, among so many bad ones.

Back in the car, engine on. Leave the lights off. Reach for the bag, rest it on my lap.

Drive.

Not down the lane. We're heading left, onto the track, down past the field, bump, bump, bump, car speeding up. Touch of the brake, just a bit. Not too fast, not yet. Bump, bump, bump. Track's getting rough. I'm starting to struggle with the wheel. But I got to hold it, got to keep us moving, and now I need more speed.

Touch of gas.

Bit more.

Faster, faster. Flash of moonlight, flash of bright water, rushing in, closer, closer, closer. One hand off the wheel, grab the bag, pull it tight. Open the door, fling it open. Bashes into a fence post, slams back at me. Kick it open again, check the track, the water, the rushing light.

Dive.

Out of the car, clutching the bag. I hit the ground, scream with the pain, roll over the track, spinning, spinning. And then I'm still. I hear the crash, feel the drops of shattered water rain upon me.

As the car plunges into the lake.

And disappears from view.

18

I STAND UP, stare down at the surface of the water. Already it's smoothing over, all traces of disturbance gone. Like the car never crashed in, like it never existed. And now everything's still again, just like it was.

Not a ripple

Just moonlight on water.

Oh, Jesus. If only I could do that with my life. Take everything that was ever bad and sink it, like I just sank that motor. Dump it in a lake, all gone in seconds, and then everything all right again.

Everything still.

Just peace and beauty.

And moonlight.

Only it doesn't work that way, does it? Not even with the car. You can sink it in a lake, hide it from view, but it's still there, isn't it? Even if no one ever finds it, you'll know it's there. It'll still exist.

But someone will find it.

Someone'll find everything you want to hide.

Cos you know what, Bigeyes? There's no secrets. Not really. I wanted to cut loose. From the knife, from the bad stuff I've done, from the past. But all I was trying to do was bury that shit. And that never works.

There's only one way to cut loose.

Really cut loose.

And this is it.

An owl calls, somewhere above me. I look back up the track. All quiet again, all still. But somewhere in the dark a bird's hunting. And now I got to go hunting too. Clasp the bag, hold it tight.

Set off up the track. Going to be hard work, even this bit up to the lane at the top of the hill. Don't ask me how I'm going to make it all the way, cos my body's hurting worse than ever. Panting already and I'm not even half-way up the slope.

Stop, take a few breaths, climb on, back to the lane, stop again. Bend over, gasp, straighten up. This could all go wrong, Bigeyes. I could hang about here for ever and still get zippo. I'm gambling the whole stack on one thing.

Hawk's anger.

I know he's mad. Oh, yeah, you bet. Question is—will he do what I think? If he does, then I got a chance. But it's all on this one throw.

Plod down the lane, into the valley. Got to stay smart, watch cute, however much I'm hurting. Going to be hooked on this road for a bit, so if a motor comes along,

I'll have to hide. Getting spotted now could sting everything.

Walk, walk.

Makes me think back to the old city, Bigeyes. Remember how I used to like walking there? I told you about it once. How it straightens my head sometimes. Funny thing is, right now, here I am walking but I don't feel I got to straighten my head. Not any more. I reckon my head's pretty well sorted.

I'm getting scared, yeah. Course I am. Scared of what's coming. Like I told you, by dawn I'm going to be choking. But that's talking heart-wise. Head-wise I feel kind of clear. Like stuff's fixed itself. Maybe it's just knowing there's nothing else to do now.

No more decisions to make.

Cos in the end, Bigeyes, it's all very simple.

You do what you got to do. It's almost like the old days. When I was given some target. I did what I had to do. No questions asked. Wait, move in, hit hard. Hit again. Only difference is, what I did then was wrong.

What I'm doing now is right.

Walk, walk.

On down the lane, on through the night.

Keep thinking of that grink's mobile in my pocket. And all the people I wish I could speak to. I don't want to use it. Don't want those grinky bastards to ever know who I rang. Pull it out, check it over.

Gone dead anyway.

What the hell was I carrying it for? Stare down at it. Wipes me out suddenly looking at it. Maybe I should have used it, taken a chance. Could have spoken while I was driving here. Might have got through to Bannerman, Ruby.

Found out what happened to 'em. And Bex.

Maybe even got through to Mary.

But I guess I'm not meant to.

I fling the phone away, go on walking. Hear the owl call again. Getting colder. I try to brisk up, put on speed, but it's hard. I'm limping so bad. Peer up at the sky. Moon's still bright, and there's stars popping out like jewels.

Lane's twisting to the left, and starting to rise again. Still no motors cutting past. All's quiet like before, just the pad of my feet as I shuffle on. Something moves over to the right, something gliding.

The owl maybe.

But it's gone.

Climb, climb. This hill's higher than the last, but it gets better after that. And worse. Cos that's when we're close to the gig. Push on, clutching the bag, panting, panting. Brow of the hill seems like it's fixed, never drawing closer.

But slowly I'm getting there, up, up, just a small distance now. Here's the top. Low stone wall this side of the lane. Stop, slump on it, breathing hard. And then check down into the next valley.

There it is, Bigeyes.

See it? Straight ahead. Don't follow the lane. It ends up where we're going but waggles off a bit first. We're not trigging that way. We're cutting off here and heading straight down the side of the valley. So forget about the lane.

Check straight ahead.

In the distance.

Surrounded by trees.

The house.

Yeah, I know. You're thinking not that big. You were expecting a mansion, right? Well, it's bigger than it looks from here, but you're right. It's not a mansion. Tell you why.

It's a retreat, a secret den, a hideaway.

A nest.

Almost no one in the world knows Hawk owns this place. Not even his family. He told me that himself. And he hardly ever comes here. Once or twice a year maybe. And then only for a special reason.

I was that special reason once.

But I didn't come here with him. That's not how it worked. I was brought here separate, by car, by one of the few grinks allowed to know about Hawk's nest. Hawk's got his own way of getting here. And I won't know till we're closer if he's turned up tonight.

Come on.

Over the stone wall, scramble down the slope, down along the valley. I'm walking faster. Don't know where the strength is coming from, but suddenly it's like I can't wait to get there. Heart's pumping too. But it's not the excitement.

It's the fear I told you about.

The house is getting closer. I can see the trees clear, see the lane bending back in from the right. Tramping through a field now, sheep munching grass all around. Look up at me with moony faces, go back to their feeding.

I trudge on.

Trees draw closer, closer. They're blocking out most of the house from this level but I can see the shadow of it beyond. No lights, far as I can tell. This could all come to nothing, Bigeyes. Into the trees, stop, catch my breath.

The bag feels so heavy now.

Like I'm carrying my whole life.

Stumble through the trees, up to the edge of the fence. Peer over at the house.

All dark. No cars outside. Nothing. Like the place is locked up for the winter. I slump against the fence, back to the house. I was wrong, Bigeyes. I screwed up. I slammed everything on one throw. And the throw came to nothing.

Then I catch it, far off.

A low drone.

I stiffen. The sound grows louder, louder. I stare up and through the treetops clap the grey form slipping through the night, over the trees, over the house. I twist round, peer over the fence. And there it is, hovering in the dark.

Hawk's copter.

And now it's coming down.

I crawl back into the trees, find the blackest spot, close up on the ground, bag tight to my chest. I can't bear to look. And it's too risky anyway. Got to just listen. I hear the whirr of the engine, the swish of the blades, then silence. No doors banging, no voices, no footsteps on the gravel.

I start to shake. He won't be alone, Bigeyes. He can fly the copter by himself but he won't be alone. He'll be protected like he always is, even in this secret place. Specially in this secret place.

I clench my fists, creep back to the fence, make myself check over.

Nobody in the copter. Lights on in the house.

And still silence.

Deep, cold silence.

Back into the trees, slump down again, stare at the bag. Feel the fear start to grow. Peer up at the sky again. I can still see the stars, Bigeyes, and the moon. And now something else.

The first streaks of light. Dawn's coming. Yeah, that's right. Another dawn I don't deserve to see. But neither does the bastard in that house. I take a long slow breath. Feel my mind clear, settle, harden. OK, Bigeyes, let's do it.

Revenge isn't sweet.

It's just necessary.

19

DAWN SKY, DEAD sky. Deep, dronky grey. Clouds, no sun. Just the dream of it, somewhere far away. But you know what, Bigeyes? I never seen a dawn so beautiful.

Take my eyes off it, stick 'em on the house.

Cos that's what matters. That's where he is. My enemy. In his castle, his nest. Hawk's nest. He's got loads of 'em, Bigeyes. You bet. All over the country, all over the world. But this one? Out here in this remote spot?

He only ever uses it for one reason. And you can probably guess what that is. If you've been paying attention. You know enough about the bastard to work out his obsession.

Yeah, OK, he's got more than one. Power, that's a big 'un. He loves that, needs it. Money, that's another. Possession, number three. You name it, he wants to own it. Antiques, paintings, boats, cars, planes, whatever. He wants the whole stack.

And people.

Oh, yeah. He's into owning people big time. And he doesn't just want part of you. He wants all of you, good and total. When he's got you like that, he's one happy boy. And one dangerous gobbo. Cos you're drummed. You don't even breathe unless he says so.

And then there's the Game.

Hawk's big obsession.

To smash up this world and build it again, in his own stinking image. Him and his fellow slime. Playing for the highest stakes of all. Yeah, he wants all that. And more. Cos you know what? There's something he aches for, Bigeyes.

And it's constant. And when things are bad, that's when he craves it most. When he's choking with anger, like he is now, that's when he's got to have it. So he comes here. To make sure he can have what he wants.

In secret.

Once upon a time, I was that secret. The reason why he came here. Not any more, thank Christ. It's some other victim now. But I can't be thinking about that. I got to stay focused.

Right, Bigeyes. Check out the house.

Go on, check it good.

All quiet. Just a few lights on. There'll be more soon. Give 'em time. They just got here, remember. Hawk's copter sitting on the gravel. No cars yet. But they'll be on their way. Hawk comes here for solitude, but it's not proper solitude.

It's solitude as he sees it.

Solitude with bodyguards.

Cop a glint over the house. Bigger than you thought, right? Looked small from a distance, I know. And it's not huge, not by Hawk's standards. Even so, it's got plenty of rooms. And there's two you got to know about.

Can't see either from here.

But you can picture 'em.

First up, look over to the right. Bottom of the house. Check out the porch. Now let your eyes flick over the gravel towards where Hawk's parked his copter. Stop just before that and let your mind dig down. Cos your eyes can't go there.

Under that very spot.

There's a bunker. Hawk had it built special. Told me himself, back in the days when I was in favour. You're thinking it's for protection. Well, maybe it was in the beginning.

But he doesn't need it for that. Not really. Got too much shit looking after him already. So he uses the bunker for something else. Yeah, Bigeyes, same again. Use your imagination.

You'll have to anyway. Cos we're not hitting the bunker. We're hitting the other room you can't see. It's hidden from here by the wing of the house. But we can't go for it now. Too dangerous. The grinks just got here so we can't snap straight in. They got their rituals. And the first ritual's to make sure the boss is safe.

So we got to pull back for a bit and . . .

Shit, sooner than I thought. Two grinks standing in the porch. I thought we'd get a few minutes to wig it but they're out here already. They'll be sniffing round the building, sheds, outhouses. And this fence I'm hiding behind.

Come on. We got to rip.

Check the bag, make sure everything's cute inside. Close it up, slip into the trees, find the darkest spot, bung a glance back. No sign of the grinks. Just glimpses of the house in the gaps between branches. But they'll grub out this little wood, no question.

I can't stay here.

On through the trees, stop at the edge, think. Got to watch my step here, Bigeyes. It's kind of thrown me, Hawk turning up same time I did. I never expected him to do that. Wasn't even sure he'd come at all.

I had two plans. If there was nobody here, I was going to break in and wait. Day, two days, whatever. Case the bastard showed. And if he was already here—like I hoped he would be—then I'd watch for a chance and snick in when I could.

Probably at night.

But now it's different, with him turning up right this second and his grinks out bumming the turf already. I got to blast out for a bit, let 'em scout round, find nothing, then pick my time and creep back.

Skirt round the trees, keep 'em between me and the house. Stone wall just ahead, snaking up the side of the valley. I had this in my head, Bigeyes, when I was trigging here. I remember it from the past.

And there's a spot up there where I think I can hide. Just hope I've remembered it good. Or guessed it good. Cos I've never hidden there before. Just seen it from the house. Anyway, let's give it a fizz.

Over to the wall, crouch close, check over. House looks older from this angle. Don't ask me why. Maybe it's the dronky grey dawn. Seems to be getting darker rather than brighter.

That might help me a bit. Got to hope so. More lights click on. Most of the downstairs rooms lit up now, couple upstairs. Here goes another. Curtains whipping back, windows opening.

And more grinks cutting into the grounds.

I don't like this, Bigeyes. The two I saw in the porch have come round and now there's two more joining 'em. Big gobbos, hard slugs. Another light goes on upstairs. Nothing on the top floor yet. All dark, curtains still drawn.

Check out the gobbos.

Talking in a group, like they're planning who checks where. I can't wait for this. Some are going to be heading this way and there's no point hanging round. But now we got more trouble.

Motors turning up, three of 'em, flash-looking slammers. Fourth motor further off, purring up the lane. They pull in, nose round Hawk's copter, stop. Clunk of doors and more beef gets out.

I'm counting fifteen.

Jesus, Bigeyes, what's happening? He never used to bring this many. Not out here. That was the whole point.

He wasn't supposed to need to. Cos this was his retreat, his little secret den. His nest, like I told you. That was what he liked best. He could get away here, keep things simple, cos only a few of his most trusted grinks knew about this place.

Only now I'm starting to get it.

And it chills my heart.

Cos it's going to make everything that much harder. Might even make it impossible. And I'm angry with myself, Bigeyes, cos I should have seen this coming. It's so bloody obvious now. Why didn't I crack it before?

Hawk's expecting grime. Course he is. I mean, face it, Bigeyes—doesn't take a buzzbrain to work it out. He's got shit flying all around him, right? The gangster bojos are blowing blood, the porkers are making arrests.

The honest porkers anyway, not the bent bastards like Jakes.

But the point is—there's enough grime out there now to make Hawk nervous. He knows they all got stuff on him. And what's worse is he knows the kid they got it from. So, yeah, even out here he's expecting trouble.

He might even be expecting me.

20

THE GRINKS ARE still standing there, naffing. Some of the beef joins 'em from the cars. Check the numbers again. Ten standing there now. Rest of the gobbos are piling into the house.

But ten's enough.

They're splitting. Two cutting off left to the sheds and outhouses, two to the barn, three round the front of the house, three off to the fence where I was hiding. And they won't stop there. They'll climb over and work through the trees.

Then check this way.

I got to shift.

And I got to keep low. Not just from the grinks outside but from the house. If I could spot the hiding place from the window, someone else can too. And cop a glint of me clambering up the valley.

Up, up, fast as I can, low as I can.

Check over my shoulder.

House is still hidden by the wall, so I reckon I'm cute from that angle, for the moment anyway. What's really bombing my head is the grinks crabbing over the fence. I can't straighten up and look for 'em. Too risky. But they'll be into the trees by now.

If I don't make it over the rise quick, they'll be out in the field and they'll have a bung-clear view up the slope. With me on it.

Christ.

Scramble on, breathing hard. Getting tired now, really tired, and the pain from where those other grinks hurt me yesterday's cranking up. Aching all over and head's thumping like it wants to break open. I grip the bag, push myself on.

Check behind again.

I can see the trees clear, and the field to the right, even the little track I cut across when I trigged here during the night. Still no figures breaking out. Jesus, Bigeyes. I just need 'em to stay in the trees a bit longer.

Few seconds, that's all.

Stay in the bloody trees.

I stumble on, up, up. Here's the top of the rise. Stumpy ground, rocky outcrops, grassy hillocks. Stone wall twists up and over the hill. Second wall branches off it to the right.

Check back.

And now there's figures below. All three gobbos. Light's picked up and I can see better. Trouble is, so can they. I drop to the ground, take a moment, lift my head, just enough to fix 'em with my eyes.

Mean-looking dregs. They'll all have guns. Not showing 'em, not here, case some farmer or local dronk comes blundering by. But they'll be armed. Trust me. Don't think any of 'em's clapped me.

Shit, they're coming up the hill.

Crawl over the edge of the rise, bundle the bag into my chest, roll down the other slope. Boulder just below to break my fall. I brace myself for the thump. Mustn't make a sound. But I can't help it. Thing slaps me so hard I give a yelp.

I lean back against the rock, catch a breath, listen. They won't have heard. It wasn't that big a yelp. Take another breath, scramble down the hill. Yeah, Bigeyes, I know what you're thinking. I'm thinking it too.

So much for the hiding place.

Well, it looked like one from the house. That's all I can say. Yeah, I know. It was a long time ago. But I remember what I saw. And it looked like there was a little gully thing just below the stone wall. Kind of a nook where I thought I could keep out of sight. Wasn't expecting this other slope to be so flat and wide open.

So there's only one thing left.

Never mind what it is. No time to explain. Down the slope, fast, fast. Got to push hard now, really hard. Moment they hit the top of the rise, they'll clap me. Unless I can get to what I've just seen.

The only place left to hide.

Trouble is, ground's rocky. One slip and I'll snag an ankle, and that's game over. Push on anyway, hard as I can.

Got to risk it. No point hanging back. Turn an ankle and I get caught. Move slow and I get caught.

So what's the point hanging back?

Got to blast down this slope.

Halfway to the bottom. Check back to the rise. No figures yet. Maybe they won't come this far. Maybe they'll just climb up part of the other side, enough to get a view round the house. Maybe that's all Hawk wants.

Yeah, right.

I'm zipping myself over with that one.

They'll hit the rise. No question. They'll do this proper. And I got to be out of sight. But here's the broken bit of the wall I spotted from the top. Scramble over it, panting hard. And here's the other thing I saw.

Gorse.

Big spiky patch. Wish it was thicker but I'll have to chance it and crawl in. It might just block the sight of me. Trouble is—I don't know. I might be easy to see. And even if I'm not, there's no other place to hide on this slope, so if the grinks are grubbing out thorough, this is the first place they'll slam.

But there's nothing I can do now. Nowhere else to go.

Onto my knees, hugging the bag with one arm, prodding a way through the spines with the other. Jesus, Bigeyes. I hate this stuff. Damp and prickly. Smells too, yuk. Check over my shoulder, peer through the spines.

Glimpses of sky, hill, the broken wall.

Too many glimpses.

This won't work, Bigeyes. If I can see out, the grinks can see in. Got to go deeper, find a place where there's no glimpses out. Trouble is, I don't know if you get that with gorse. Specially this time of year. It looked thick from up top but down here, in the middle of it, I'm crawling about and crawling about and I still feel like any neb with half an eye can see me.

Here's a better clump.

Thicker, darker. More prickly, more smelly, but who cares? It's all that's left. And now I got no choice. Got to stay right where I am and not move. Cos there's voices coming close.

Gobbos.

Got to be those three grinks. Can't see 'em. I'm curled up, tight as I can, bag locked against my chest, back to the wall. And the voices are coming from there. Don't ask me if they can see me through the gorse, cos I don't know. And I don't dare move my head to look. Got to just trust now.

And hope.

Voices getting louder, footsteps tramping nearer. Then everything stops. And suddenly there's nothing. Just me curled up, in the gorse, in the silence.

Waiting.

Like them.

Just a few feet away.

I can feel 'em. They haven't climbed over the wall, but they're close. Don't ask me how I know. Leaning on the rubbly brick, I'm guessing, looking over, checking the gorse. Checking me, maybe. Grinning to each other at the sight of the kid curled up in the gorse, thinking no one can see him.

Sound of a chuckle, another. Burst of sniggering, then a scramble of feet, grunts. They're making their way over the broken wall. No mistaking that. Tramping again, swish of gorse, somewhere behind me.

Then a voice.

'Top field. Just down from the wall. The gorse.'

I'm shivering now. Can't stop it. I stay curled up, tight as I can. Nothing else to do. No point moving. But I want to look round. I want to fix 'em, if only to glare back. Voice comes again.

'Yeah, OK.'

He's talking on a phone.

I take a breath, force myself to stay still. More tramping, circling the gorse now. Flick my eyes about, peer into the spines. Nothing clear to see, just shadowy forms edging round. The voices have stopped. Then I catch a new sound. And I recognize it straight up.

The copter. It's taking off. I curl up tighter, listen. Sound's getting louder, closer. I look up and catch a new shadowy form, hovering over me like a great bird. Laughter again, hooting even.

I clench my fists. Yeah, you bastards. You're loving this, aren't you? The easiest job you ever had. Stroll up the hill, down the other side, and there's the kid, shivering in the gorse.

Waiting for you.

Hawk's going to love you boys so much.

The bird-shadow looms closer. Hasn't landed yet. Still hovering, but it's getting lower all the time. I stare up.

Still hard to make the thing out with all these spiny little branches in the way. But I don't need to.

I can picture everything.

And right now I'm picturing a face. Hawk's face. He'll be at the controls. Oh yeah, you bet. The grinks probably spotted me here from the top of the rise, rang the house, sauntered down.

And the big man's come in person. Like he would.

He's in that copter right now. I know it.

And I'm dead.

21

COPTER MOVES CLOSER. It's not just the engine getting louder, the shadow getting bigger. It's the spines of the gorse. They're dancing in the rushing draught. More laughter from the gobbos, more hooting.

I curl up tighter. Don't know why I'm bothering. Might as well lie on my back, wait for 'em to pluck me out. Cos they can't miss me, not now. The gorse is swaying, bouncing, over me, round me, gaps opening on all sides. I'm like water pouring out of a sieve.

I think of the bag, what's in it. If I'd been quicker, got myself ready, I could have used that. Now it's a wasted gig. The gobbos down here'll see what I'm doing and stiff me before I can prime up. Before the copter gets down, before Hawk even gets out.

But nobody grabs me.

Nobody even touches me.

And there's a change in the sound above me.

The copter's not coming down. I can tell from the buzz of the engine. It's climbing again. I whip a glance up. It's turned back into a shadow, cos the gorse has closed round me again. The other shadows are moving too, some disappearing, some cutting round after the others.

And suddenly there's no shadows at all.

No voices, no laughter. Just the drone of the copter, fading.

And the gorse lying still.

I'm trembling bad, squeezing the bag tight like before. I don't get it, Bigeyes. They must have seen me. They can't be blind. I take a breath. Too scared to move. I don't feel safe here but it's all I got. I want to just stay curled up, in this spiny darkness. But I can't.

I got to know what's happened.

Push back the branches, peer through.

I counted wrong. There's twelve of 'em. But maybe some came up from the house separate, climbed over that other wall. Yeah, there's a stile. They probably trigged over that way.

Whatever.

Twelve of the bastards.

And they're heading off right, backs to me.

Copter's wigged it over the house, hovering over the fields on the other side. Check back to the gobbos. Still walking on, but spreading out now, covering the ground all the way up to the top wall and down to the base of the valley.

I can only guess what happened.

They missed me, Bigeyes. They just bloody missed me. Came this way to grub out the place. Normal routine. Hawk always makes his dronks do that. Gathered round the gorse, had a few laughs. Copter comes over, checking too.

Grinks in the copter fly down, hover over the gorse. Bit of larking with the dronks on the ground. Nobody's checking the gorse. Cos they're all looking at each other. Copter flies off. Gobbos on the ground trig on.

Just guessing.

Whatever happened, I was lucky. And I got another slam at this thing. Problem is, I can't stay here. Got away with it once but it's too risky. They should have smacked the gorse. They will next time. Probably poke it about.

I got to pull back, find another place to hide, wait there till dark. Yeah, Bigeyes. We got to be patient. There's that many grinks swilling round, I'll never get past 'em in daylight.

Hawk's nervous. That's clear. Never seen so many minders round this place. And he won't have been in the copter. I was wrong about that. He'll be holed up in the house, making sure he's safe. Then waiting for his treat to be brought to the bunker.

I got to play this cute.

Check out through the spines. Copter's way off to the right, grinks still ploughing on, backs to me. Clutch the bag, crawl back through the gorse, check out the broken wall. Nobody standing there, nobody near. Nobody I can see anyway.

I got to go for it, Bigeyes.

Out of the gorse, keeping low, scramble over the break in the wall, crouch against the other side, check round. Nobody up on the rise, nobody in this part of the valley. Bung a glance up the far hill. Looks like a fence running along the top.

Don't ask me what's behind it.

Just got to hope there's somewhere I can go to ground, stay out of sight, crack out the hours till dark. Down the hill, low, close to the wall. Ground's rocky like before but it's getting mushier with every step.

Bottom of the valley. Little stream trickling along it. Never saw that from the top. Kick through it, up the other side towards the fence. Check behind. Still nobody watching from the opposite hill.

But I'm choking about that copter. Can't see it but it sounds closer than it was. Think it's heading back towards those other grinks. Jesus, Bigeyes. I got no chance if it rips over here.

Engine's getting louder. I push against the wall, twist my head. Still no sign of it. Creep on, up the hill towards the top. Copter's hovering, somewhere over the field beyond the wall. I keep moving, up, up, up.

Top of the hill's getting closer. Fence is clear to see now and it's a whack to climb, thank Christ. Just hope I can get to it without being clapped. On, on, tight to the wall.

Sound of the engine changes again. Now's the moment. Copter's spinning back towards the house. Push on up the slope, stop at the fence. This is where it gets scary, Bigeyes. Cos they can see me best up here.

Ease my head up, check over the wall.

The grinks I saw earlier are trigging back towards the gorse. Watch close, Bigeyes. See? I was right. They smack the gorse, poke through it. Move on towards the break in the wall.

This is it. Got to move now. Before they hit this part of the valley. Slime up the fence, low as I can, ease over the top, down the other side, duck below the level of the rise.

Check what's in front of me.

And oh, you beauty. Another valley—and trees. Nice big patch too. Come on, Bigeyes. Down the slope, steady, steady. Got to watch my footing. Still rocky ground. But it's flattening out quicker than the other slope, and here's the first of the trees already. Dive into the dark, pick a path through the gloom.

Yeah, just what I want. Trees tight together. We'll find a spot on the far side. Stuff as much turf as we can between us and the grinks. Don't suppose they'll come grubbing out here. They'll check for grime close to the house, make sure everything's cute for Lord H, then pull back.

And watch.

All the time.

Yeah, Bigeyes. It's going to be a bum gripe getting into Hawk's nest. But I'm going for it. I'm telling you. I haven't come all this way just to blast off again cos it's a spitty gig. I got one reason for being here. And no reason for being anywhere else.

Here's a good spot.

Big, tall trees, close-packed, high canopies. Not much in the way of leaves, but I can't help that. Wrong bloody season to be doing this. Check round. Got to choose the best one.

This'll do. Bastard to climb cos there's no low branch and the trunk's got nothing to snag onto. Yeah, Bigeyes, you got it.

I want a bastard to climb. So no one'll expect to see me up there.

And this one's a proper dingo.

Come on.

22

OPEN THE BAG, check through. Still can't believe it, Bigeyes—Ezi giving me everything I asked for. Didn't think I'd get the plum shit, never mind the other stuff. But it's all in the bag. Bless his wicked heart.

Pull out the rope, check it over. Light, strong, just like I wanted. Tie a few stop-knots at one end, give it some weight. Peer up, fix the bottom branch, aim, chuck. Rope curls over first go, loops down the other side. Flick the rope a few times, ease the weighted end further down, reach up, grab it.

Hook the rope through the bag handles, tie the ends together, check everything's firm. Squeeze the rope-lines into one, take a breath, haul myself up, slow, steady. No need to rush. And just as well.

I'm panting already.

Jesus, Bigeyes, this is tough. I used to be great at climbing. I probably still am. You don't lose that. But I'm feeling the strain bad. Head's still pounding. So's my body. It's almost like I forgot the pain when I was trying to get away from those dungpots back there.

Now there's no grinks, the pain's blamming me again.

Push on, up the rope. Got to reach that first branch. It's easy after that. And I can stay hidden up there, hopefully. Just got to reach that first branch. On, on, closer, closer. Here's it is, just a bit further.

Reach up, clap hold of the branch.

Bark feels cold, unwelcoming. But I don't care. Drag myself up the last few inches, flop over onto the branch, lie there, gasping. Then I hear it again.

The sound of the copter.

Buzzing close. Check up through the canopy. Bits of the sky visible but not much. I chose good with this tree. But I better stay down here for the moment, let the copter skip past. Peer down.

Bag's swinging at the bottom of the rope. Haul it up, slip it free, coil the rope, stuff it back in the bag. Check up again. Copter's over the trees now but it's off to the left. No way they can see me down here. Long as they don't come any nearer.

But it's OK. They're flying off already towards the house.

And I'm moving too, up, up. I've seen what I want, right near the top. Check it out, Bigeyes. See the bit I mean? OK, we'll get a bit closer. Up, up, nice and slow. Right, here we are. See it now?

Proper little snug. Well, all right. Not a snug. A snug's somewhere comfy. Warm and safe with food and a good bed. And books. Jesus, yeah. Books. I bloody miss books.

So I guess this isn't a snug. But I'll tell you what, Bigeyes.

It's the nearest thing we got out here.

And it's not bad. Little cradle of branches to hold me firm. I could fall asleep up here and not slip out. But I won't be falling asleep. No chance of that. I'm too cold, too cranked up. Too frightened.

That's right, Bigeyes. No point zipping you over. I'm choked out. Ease myself into the cradle, lean back, pull the bag onto my chest.

Close my eyes.

Yeah, my friend. I'm scared like I've never been scared before. Freaked out of my brain. I suppose I shouldn't be. Cos think about it. I mean, I've done what I'm doing so many times.

And I was younger back then. Dead young. But I still went out and did the business. Hawk would give me some target. Just a name, bit about where to find the bastard, anything I needed to know to slam the gig.

Then leave the rest to me.

So how many times have I waited like this? Eh? Lost count. Honest, Bigeyes, I've lost count. Yeah, I know. You're thinking about the list I wrote for Bannerman, all the dronks I killed. You're thinking there's the number. Count that.

But I can't. Cos there's more.

There's the targets I never hit. I went for 'em, planned the gig, set it up, waited like this, and never got lucky. For whatever reason. I was good, Bigeyes, but I didn't plug every dronk I went for. And when I failed, I paid for it with Hawk.

Oh yeah, you bet.

But here's the point. I've been here before. Lots of times. Waiting, thinking, feeling scared. So why's this different? Yeah, dimpy question. Don't know why I'm even asking. Cos it's easy as piss to tell you.

It's different cos of the target. Cos it's Hawk. And it's different cos of the other thing. The thing that chewed Ezi up when I told him what I need. The thing I got in this bag. It's different cos of that.

I'm scared, Bigeyes.

Almost too scared to move.

But I'll tell you one thing. I'm clear about what's right. What I got to do, what I must do, what I bloody will do. Long as I can find the spit. If anything's going to make me move, it'll be that.

Knowing what's right.

Take a breath, a long breath. Keep my eyes closed. Feel the pain go on, in my body, in my heart. Yeah, that's it, Bigeyes. Knowing what's right. But here's something. When did I start knowing what that was?

When I met Becky? Cos you bet she told me. Oh, yeah. She was just like Ruby for talking straight. Only it didn't work, did it? Cos I kept on doing what was wrong. So maybe it didn't come from Becky. I heard what she said but I took no notice.

So when did I know, eh? I mean, when did I know proper? When I met Mary? Or Jaz?

Can't answer that, Bigeyes. But you know what I'm starting to think? I reckon I knew the answer long before. From the moment I was born almost. I knew it was wrong I got no memory of my parents. That they dumped me outside that stinky home. I knew it was wrong what happened to me inside.

And afterwards.

Specially with Hawk.

I knew that was wrong. All of it. Didn't need someone to come and tell me. And that's my point, Bigeyes. You know right and you know wrong. You're born knowing it. Question is—how do you deal with what you know?

Can't answer that either.

All I know is—I didn't deal with it good. Didn't deal with anything good. If I had done, I wouldn't be here, shivering in a tree. Hungry, cold, hurting, scared.

Getting ready to kill.

Again.

Another breath. Another shiver.

I'm freezing up, Bigeyes. And I don't just mean in my head. Pull the coat tight round me. Should have done this better. Should have got more food inside me before I plugged the car in the lake. There was a place back there I could have called at, just before I hit the country lanes. Maybe got some soup.

But I wasn't thinking.

I just wanted to get here, see if Hawk had showed.

But there's no point glumming. Got to bottle up and get through today. Open my eyes, look round. Tips of the branches moving. Sound of a bird singing off to the right. Don't know what type. Peer round into the trees beyond. Singing goes on but I can't see where it's coming from.

Gone quiet now.

No sounds anywhere. Just the fear murmuring inside me. Touch of rain on my face. Look up, let it patter over me. Feels cold but it's only light. Shouldn't be a problem, long as it doesn't last. Tuck the bag inside my coat to keep it dry.

Close my eyes again. Got to rest now, Bigeyes. Got to get calm, get cool, focus. Cos I'm not going to sleep. No chance of that. But I'm wrong. I fall asleep like I'm wrapped up in a blanket. And I stay asleep, a long, long time.

When I wake, the rain's stopped and there's mist all around.

And voices at the base of the tree.

23

GOBBOS. NO PRIZES for guessing what kind. Twist my head, check down. Three figures standing there. Yeah, grinks, no question. Not looking up. Don't think they've clapped me. Not acting like they have. I'm guessing they're just grubbing round like before.

But this is close.

Got to just hope I chose the right tree. Like I told you, it's a bastard to climb, so they might just slop past without checking up. But if they're doing their job cute, they'll cop a glint this way.

Still standing there, peering round, ground level. I hold my breath, watch. Good thing I'm high up but I'm still visible, even with the mist down.

Move on, you clapheads.

They don't. Just stand there, bottom of the tree, one of 'em munching an apple. I recognize him now. He stamped through the gorse earlier. More voices—shit. Coming from the left. Gobbo with the apple calls out.

'Over here!'

Mutter from the other voices, and now I see 'em. Two more gobbos. Heavy dronks. Jesus, Bigeyes. This is bad. Got to keep still as I can. Only now there's a bird chirping up. Bloody robin, sitting on the next branch. I glare at him.

Cut it out, birdy.

He doesn't.

I peer down at the grinks. All five together now, same spot. Someone's got to look up any moment. I make my body small as I can. Grinks go on naffing, robin goes on chirping. Then a shout below.

'There! Up in the tree!'

I stiffen.

Guffaws below, a big throaty sound. I don't dare look. Just start shivering. Sound of a shot, another. Nothing hits me. Robin flies off. And then there's silence.

But only for a second. Guffaws again, hard, brutal. I make myself peer down. And there they are, all the grinks together, playing football.

With a dead squirrel.

I twist my head back, make myself even smaller. The laughter goes on, then fades away. I wait, go on waiting. No more sounds below. I take a breath. Got to look again, Bigeyes. Got to force myself.

I hesitate, check down.

No sign of the grinks.

Just the squirrel, lying still.

The robin flutters back. Doesn't bother singing. Just perches there, fixes me, stays quiet. I lean back in the cradle, peer round. The branches are dewy and the colour's fading from 'em.

Air feels still.

Like it's scared too.

I clench my fists. I feel so weak, so helpless. But there is one thing on my side—the mist. And night's coming on. Yeah, Bigeyes. I slept through most of the day. Don't ask me how that happened. But I did it. So I guess this is it.

No holding back.

It's time to hit the gig.

Check down, listen. No sign of the grinks, no sound either. I give it five minutes, ten, fifteen—but now I'm bottling. One last check—all quiet below. Darker too, mistier.

Look round for the robin.

Gone. Never saw him wig it. Too bad. I wanted to say goodbye.

Stretch my arms, legs, pull the bag out from under the coat. Climb back down to the lowest branch, feed the rope ends round it, through the handles of the bag, tie 'em together, let everything fall. Wait a moment, grab the rope, squeeze, shin down to the ground.

Squirrel's by my right foot. I bend down, look it over. Half its head blown off by the bullet. I feel the tears come. Don't know why. I should be able to crack this. But then I get it.

The fluffy little toy.

Squirrel Nutkin.

Jaz had a Squirrel Nutkin. Last time I saw her. Last time I'll ever see her.

I straighten up quick, flick my eyes off the corpse. Got to move, got to act. It's not a time for crying. Not now, not ever again. Untie the rope ends, hook the bag free, drop it on the ground.

Stare at it.

Take a breath.

Feel the stillness in the air. Rope's still loose over the branch, both ends hanging down. Not moving, not swaying, not even a bit. I reach out, snap one end tight in my hand, pull. Whole thing comes wriggling down, falls in a heap over the bag and the dead squirrel.

Feel the stillness again. And the fear.

Bend down, coil up the rope, rest it back on the ground. Pick up the bag, open it, look inside. It's all in here, Bigeyes. Everything I need now. My past, my present, my future.

All in this bag.

Tip it up, empty everything out, stare down.

I'm breathing too fast. I should be calm, in control, like I used to be. Even when I was scared, I made sure I was in control. I take a moment, make myself breathe slow, force it, in, out. Count, you claphead. Count the seconds, count the breaths.

Slowing down a bit.

Not enough but a bit.

I go on counting breaths, in, out, in, out. Stare round at the trees. Dark and misty, yeah, yeah. Just how I want you. Just how I want everything. A last slow breath, heave it in, heave it out.

Now forget about breathing.

Get your stump moving.

Bend down, check everything over. Going to take a few minutes, Bigeyes. Got to make sure everything's as it should be. But Ezi was right. It's no big deal handling this kit. Anyone could do it. Even you.

But I take my time.

Oh, yeah. I'm doing this right, Bigeyes. I'm taking all the time I need to get ready. Five minutes, ten minutes. Last check over. One more for luck. OK, I'm cute to go.

Bag's empty now. Got everything I need on me. Just the rope to sort out. Tie it round my waist, stuff the bag under some leaves. Straighten up, see the squirrel lying there. Bend down again, look over the body.

It's so dark and still. Hard to think it ever had life inside it. I feel the ghosts come back. The pictures I can't bear to see. I reach down, touch the fur. Think of Jaz again.

Stand up, trembling.

'Move,' I mutter.

Last check over the kit. All in place.

'Move,' I say again.

And I'm off, into the darkness, into the mist.

24

AND SUDDENLY IT'S like I'm awake. Like I've been asleep, deep deep under, and I've just woken up, and I'm sharp and quick and ready. Like all my senses have spiked up. Now the gig's started proper.

The old excitement.

The fear, the energy.

I'm still scared. But I'm better now I'm moving, now I'm hunting. And I got big prey. Something I want bad. Through the trees, mist all around now, and getting thicker and mingled with the dark.

I like this.

Yeah, I like it very much.

Voices off to the right. Funny how they don't scare me like they did just now. I shouldn't feel safe down here on the ground, but I do. Somehow I know I can keep out of their way.

Walk on, soft, easy. It's all coming back, Bigeyes. Just like the old days. I was choking up in the tree. No question.

Choking my head to bits. But I'm cool as a knife edge now. Cool as a blade. Cool as Blade even.

Yeah, cool as Blade.

Voices getting nearer. I stop, crouch, listen. Still don't feel scared. It's like fear's just blasted out. I'm crouching and listening, and the grinks are getting nearer, and I'm still not scared. Cos I just know they won't see me.

Here they come.

Four gobbos. Can't see 'em, but I can sense 'em. And the number of 'em. It's not just the voices. It's the whole feel of 'em. Yeah, Bigeyes, I got my instinct coming back. And about time too.

Cos I need it.

Shadows in the trees, off to the right. Yeah, I know. Looks like one big blobby bastard. Well, it's four grinks. Don't ask me how I know. I just do. Come on. We're splitting right.

Round the side of the oak, crouching. Shadows pass, disappear. I move on. Can't believe how spiked up I am. Feel like I can do anything. And I need this confidence. Cos there's big grime waiting for us.

Left, round the back of where those gobbos came from. Going to have to watch cute. Watch behind, I mean. Cos those dungpots are going to be coming back at some point. So I got to keep a glint over my stump.

But we're all right for now.

On through the trees, and now we're coming to the edge. Stop by the open ground, check round. All I can see is mist and darkness. But I know where the hill is, and the fence at the top.

Up that way, see?

Never mind how I worked it out. Come on.

Into the murk, slow, slow. Can't even see the ground, so I got to watch my step. Ground's starting to rise. What did I tell you? We're climbing and the fence'll be at the top.

Taking an age getting up. Thought we'd be there by now. But no sign of the fence. And now there's voices again. And it's not the gobbos who passed behind us. It's more, and they're somewhere in front.

I'm guessing the other side of the fence.

Stop, listen.

Got to wait. Can't make out where they're coming from. They might not even be moving. Which case I got to be careful. I could walk straight into 'em if I get this wrong.

But there we go again. My old instincts. I got the grinks now, like I'm seeing 'em clear, spite of the mist. They're almost straight in front, just a bit to the right, and they're not moving. Just blobbed there, naffing.

Got a feeling they came out with the gobbos we just saw. Probably Hawk sent 'em out for another grub round. I cut left, up the slope, and here's the fence. Stop again, listen.

Voices off to the right now. Can't see anyone. Just a cloud of mist and dark, and the fence close by, damp under my hand. I go on listening. They're moving. Yeah, definitely moving. Towards the fence.

But not where I am.

I climb over, quick, quiet, drop down the other side. Stop again, listen. Just one voice now. Carries easy. Piece of piss to work out what's going on. He's talking on a mobile to one of the gobbos we saw earlier.

I push on, down the slope to the bottom of the valley, stop. Voices gone quiet. Can't tell if they've climbed over the fence or they're coming back this way. Got to watch myself, Bigeyes. Pretty sure they're not following but I better not hang about.

Left, over to the wall, follow it up the other side of the slope. Here's the broken bit. Climb through it, past the gorse, on, on. That's right, Bigeyes. We're keeping away from the trees we hid in when we first got here. I'm hitting the house from the other side.

More voices—stop, listen again. Different ones. Near too. I crouch down. Still mist and dark all around but I know where I am. I'm in the next field and halfway up the last slope. Top of that there's a wall and then it's down to the house in the dip below.

But that's where these new voices are coming from.

I'm listening cute as I can.

Can't work out how many nebs there are. Just know there's lots. And they're closing in. Left, down to the bottom of the valley, cut along straight, back up the slope towards the wall. Ground's bad here, worse than the other slopes. Got to pick my way over rocks I can't see.

And the mist's getting worse.

Voices moving to the right, down to the spot where I last was. I'm sensing at least five grinks. That means there's lots outside now. The four we first heard, then the ones up by the fence, and now these five. And Christ knows how many others Hawk's sent out.

Jesus, Bigeyes.

He's scared.

He's really scared.

I keep moving, up the last slope. More rocks, more bloody rocks, but I'm getting close. Feeling the weight now, the burden of what I'm carrying. Didn't feel it till now. Don't know why. I kind of forgot it with all these grinks to watch out for.

But the slope's taking it out of me, I'm breathing hard.

And I'm feeling the bloody weight.

Stop, take a moment, get my strength back a bit. Got to stay quiet, stay slick. Cos this is where it cranks up. Here's the wall. And after that there's nothing between us and the house.

Except a few hundred grinks.

Yeah, yeah. Not that many. But enough, OK? Even with all these other bastards outside. There'll be plenty more close to the building. And inside. Hawk's brought a bloody regiment with him. I'm guessing more's turned up while I was sleeping up in the tree.

Stop at the wall, listen again.

No voices. But I'm sensing grinks again. Somewhere near. Can't tell if they're right or left or middle. Just know there's nebs close by. Got 'em. Shadows to the left.

See 'em?

Crouch behind the wall, edge over to a gap in the stonework, peer through. Two grinks. No, three. Carrying guns. Beam of a torch flashes round towards me. I duck, let it pass over. Hear the tramp of their feet in the spongy grass.

Heading the other way.

Straighten up, check round. Run my hands over the wall. Got to watch this bit. Looks crumbly and if a stone crunches out when I'm climbing, some grink might hear it. I test a few stones.

Too risky. Too loose.

More to the right, check again.

This bit's cute.

Up the side, steady, slow. Yeah, you beauty. Nice, firm rock. Just make sure you stay like that. I reach the top, check round, jump down the other side, land soft.

Check again.

Mist swirling, darkness swirling.

But now something else down below.

The lights of the house.

25

I FEEL MY senses spice up even more. I clench my fists, flex my muscles. I never felt so sharp, so ready. I start to move, slow, down towards the house.

No sign of the building itself. Not yet. Just the lights, and now they're gone. Mist's closed round again. But I got a glimpse, enough to see what's where. And I don't mean the house. I knew where that was anyway.

I'm talking about the part I got to hit.

Cos there's only one way I'm getting in.

I worked it out way back. No question how to snap this. Go straight to him. And I'm not talking about the bunker, Bigeyes. That's where he'll be lots of the time. Maybe he's there now, having his sick fun with some poor shit.

But I'm not talking about that.

I'm talking about where he goes later. By himself. The place where he's always alone. He has to have that place.

I know cos he told me, one day when his tongue was loose. He told me he had to have that place. Everywhere he owns, he's got to have one special place.

Where it's just him.

And no one else allowed.

Except me. Yeah, Bigeyes, that's the stinger. He let me in there. Just a few times. When I was in favour. If you can call it that. I don't want to talk about it. But it wasn't often anyway. Like I say, it's his private place. And I'll tell you something, Bigeyes.

He'll need that place right now. Oh yeah, real bad. I know that cos I know him good. That's why he's come out here. To this remote spot. Cos it's got the two things he wants most. The bunker where he can give out pain—in secret. And the other place.

Where he can rest and plan.

And stay safe.

Alone.

Trust me, Bigeyes. He needs 'em both right now. He's under pressure like he's never been before. Specially now the porkers and the gangster bojos are hitting big. So when he's done with the bunker and sent off the poor bastard he's been whamming in there, he'll head for the other place.

And he'll need that more than ever.

Specially with all these grinks spilling round him. I mean, he wants 'em, yeah, for safety. But don't kid yourself. They're just robots to him. He just uses 'em cos he needs 'em. But deep down, you know what? He hates 'em. Every single one of 'em. They're the same thing to him as they are to you and me.

Scum.

So he'll use 'em for smashing the fields, grubbing for danger. Protection, torture, killing, whatever. But they're nothing to him. Like most nebs are nothing to him. Even his family. Yeah, I mean it. Even them.

Cos that's how it really is, Bigeyes. The only person he loves is himself. So for all his power over other people, he's got no one. No bloody one. Yeah, he owns these grinks, like he owns pretty much everybody in his life. But deep down, he's on his own, trusting no one, hating everyone.

Knowing in his heart they hate him too.

Cos they do. Oh yeah.

Don't ask me how I know.

He's better off dead, Bigeyes.

There's the lights again. I'm just where I want to be. Still no sign of the buildings but the lights tell me what I want to know. Main building's to the right. So we're cutting left, between the outhouses and the stable.

And we got to go cute, cos I'm sensing more grinks nearby.

Yeah, I was right. Cop that shadow. Got it? Never mind, too late. Take it from me. Big guy, just got a glimpse of him. Carrying a rifle. Walk on, low, slow. More shadows—stop.

They're dead ahead, not moving.

Lights behind 'em, twinkling a bit. Gone. Can't see the shadows either but I'm sensing they're still there. Move right, just a bit, now straight on. Got to squeeze round these bastards.

Sound of tramping, off to the left.

Moving away.

But now there's more steps coming from the right. Freeze, crouch, wait. Three grinks plod past, beefbums. Two got rifles, third's carrying a torch. They don't see me, walk on. I let 'em go, wait, move on, closer to where the lights were.

Squashy ground comes to an end and now there's mown grass.

First of the stables. No horses in there now. Hawk used to keep 'em and yeah—you guessed it—he's a brilliant rider. As you'd expect. Brilliant at everything. Brilliant rider, brilliant shot, brilliant whatever.

But he stopped keeping horses here cos he doesn't use the place often enough. And right now I'm glad, cos I can do without snorting noises as I slip past. Up to the first door, check in.

No grinks.

On towards the first of the outhouses. More foot-steps, left and right. I freeze again, listen. None of 'em coming this way. Trig on, past the first outhouse, past the second. Shadow of the barn opens up on my left.

And there on my right's the outline of the main building.

I can see it good now, lights on in most of the rooms. I keep low. Don't think anyone can clap me from the windows cos I'm still swirled in mist and darkness, but I got to play stealth.

Keep back, edge round the building. Barn slips from view and now I'm close to the drive and forecourt. I'm not slamming in this way. Wouldn't make it past the porch. But there's something I got to check. Cos I need to know numbers.

Rough-cut, I mean.

Trig on, low, up to the edge of the house, peer round.

Forecourt opens up. Misty and dark like everything else but there's lights on all around and I can see enough. Hawk's copter's sitting there, and more motors than there were. Loads more. I was right, Bigeyes.

He's got an army keeping watch.

Run my eye back to the copter. And the ground nearby.

Think of the bunker underneath.

Pull back, creep round to where the barn opened up. But now we're keeping close to the house. This is the tough part, Bigeyes, the really tough part. Cos I got lots to do and there's that many grinks here some screamer's bound to drum in and spot me.

So I got to choose the right moment.

And move quick.

Here's the place. Check round. What do you see? Yeah, I know—mist and darkness. And the house. Look again. Look better. OK, point one—no windows. So no one can peer out at me. Point two—look up, Bigeyes.

What do you see?

The wall of the house, climbing, all the way to something you never spotted first time round. And you won't see it now cos of the mist and the dark. But it's there. A little tower at the top of the building. All on its own, built special.

A nest, Bigeyes.

A sanctuary for a dangerous man.

Let's go get him.

26 OVER TO THE wall, crouch close, whip a glance round. No shadows moving nearby, but voices left and right. Grinks still grubbing round. Can't tell if they're sliming this way. Don't think so.

Wait, make sure.

Cos if I go at the wrong time, I'm plugged. I won't even get close to where I got to be. Like I said. I got to choose the right moment. No mistakes. And then blast off quick.

The voices go on. Not getting closer. Not moving away either. Part of me wants to wait, stay low. But that's a dronky choice too. Cos they could clap me just as easy here too, even in the murk.

I'm going for it.

Flick a glance up the wall of the building. Yeah, I know. You're thinking, bastard to climb, nothing to hold on to. And you'd be right. But bang your head back, Bigeyes.

Remember that dingo tree and the first branch? Way out of reach but get to it and everything's cute.

Now look up the building again.

Smooth brick all the way but then—yeah, baby. Little bit of the wall jutting out. Got it? Gargoyle thing on the end. Water runs out of it from that drainpipe above. Building's got loads of stony figures like that. If you look close. But we don't need to.

We just got to hit that one ugly beast. Cos he's our first branch, right? Get to him and we're close to stuff I can climb. Another glance round.

Voices have gone quiet. I don't like that. Didn't hear 'em move off so those grinks could be anywhere. Take a breath, another, try to calm down, brace up.

OK, let's do it.

Check over the kit, make sure everything's in its place. Uncoil the rope, tighten the stop-knots at the end. Tie a couple more. Going to need more punch than last time, cos this throw's a bum blitz.

Might not even work at all. Gargoyle's higher up than the branch of that tree. And harder to loop over. And even if I do hook it, the thing might snap under my weight. That's something else I'm trying not to think about.

Stand up, glint round into the mist. All's still, far as I can tell. Take a step back from the wall, check up, swing the rope, swing the rope, swing the rope.

Chuck.

Falls short.

Well short.

Voices again, moving close this time. Slink back to the wall, crouch, wait. They move close, then fade again, heading towards the barn. Stand up, out again, check up, swing the rope.

Up it goes. Falls short like before.

Nowhere near. Now I'm getting worried. Not cos of the rope. I got enough, no question. I gave Ezi the length and he did good, gave me what I wanted. No, Bigeyes, I'm worried about me.

Having the strength.

Cos I'm reeling again.

And it's not just throwing this thing. It's what comes after. The climb. And then the gig itself. Don't ask me how I'm going to manage. I was feeling sharp a moment ago. I'm not now.

Check up again, fix the jutty part of the wall. I can see the gargoyly shape at the end, even in the gloom. Figure of a boy, screaming. Could almost be me. I narrow my eyes, swing the rope.

The rope snakes up, up, up. Slaps the gargoyle, falls back. But this one was close. Gather in the line, get ready, fix the spot, swing. Up it goes, up, up, loops over the gargoyle, dangles over the neck of the figure, stops.

I take a breath, listen for sounds behind me. No voices, nothing. I want to check over my shoulder cos I still don't feel right. But I don't dare take my eyes off the rope case it slips off.

I stare at it.

Flick the rope.

A little wave rolls up it, all the way to the top, nudges the hanging end down a bit. I see the stop-knots swinging in the dark. Another flick, another little wave ripples up the line and down the other side.

Flick again, and again. Got to play this careful. Flick too big and the rope'll fall off. But it's cute so far, and the stop-knots are falling easy.

Down, down, nice and slow.

Come on, you beauty. Just a bit more.

Closer, closer, the rope still plum over the gargoyle, the knotted end almost in reach.

'Hey! What you doing?'

Gobbo's voice behind me.

I let go of the rope, whirl round, fists clenched. But all I see's mist and dark. No figure anywhere. Footsteps off to the right, tramping this way. I reach for the rope. Got to pull it down before they see it.

But there's no time.

Two shadows moving in from the right.

I scuttle in to the wall, crouch low as I can. Two gobbos, big guys, tanking round the side of the house. They can't miss seeing me. Or the rope at least. It's just hanging there. But they're staring the other way, into the mist.

One of 'em calls out. Same voice I just heard.

'What you doing? And where are you?'

'Over here,' comes an answer. 'Checking the barn.'

And the two grinks disappear from view.

I'm out from the wall, smart. That's it, Bigeyes. Can't wait a moment longer. I got lucky with the gorse. And up in the tree. And now this. But it won't happen again.

Back to the rope, grab hold, calm myself, look up.

Flick, flick, tiny waves shivering up to the top, and still the line stays cute on the jutting wall. And the other end drops lower, lower. Another flick and it's mine. I reach out.

Stop, check myself.

I want to snatch it so bad. But I mustn't. I got to watch every movement, Bigeyes. It could flip off the gargoyle easy. I take a moment, spice my head, check round again. All clear. Take the rope, hold it soft.

Tie both ends together, squeeze the two parts into one line, hold it tight in my fist. Look up, give a tug. Feels firm up there. Pull harder, harder. Nothing gives. So far so good.

Trouble is, I can't see what the top's looped over. I'm hoping it's the hollow in the back of the figure's neck. That should keep it snug. But I can't see for sure. Just got to hope it doesn't slip off when I'm climbing. So I mustn't wriggle about too much.

Anyway, let's go.

Up the rope, shinning slow. I'm trying not to move jerky but it's hard. Least the gargoyle's holding me good. Up, up, up. Check down.

The ground's already disappearing in mist.

More voices below. Can't tell where they're coming from. Seem to be in lots of places at once. Check up again. Halfway there. I'm moving faster than I meant to but I can't help myself. I'm so choked about getting seen from the ground.

Trouble is, the speed's making me swing a bit.

Slow down. For Christ's sake, slow down.

I'm still swinging.

Stop, wait, let the rope stop swinging.

Climb on. Up, up, nice and slow, and here's the little gargoyle. Like I told you, a screaming boy. Like looking at myself. Reach up, hook a hand over the stony back. Thicker than it looks from the ground, thank God.

Haul myself over, sit astride, breathe hard, check below. Rope's swinging in the mist. Check up. And there's more mist waiting.

And somewhere in it, Hawk's nest.

27

HAUL UP THE rope, untie the ends, coil it round me, crawl along the stone to where it meets the wall. Drainpipe running up to the next level— the roof of the main building. No problem getting that far.

It's the last bit that's going to slam me.

If I get it wrong.

But first things first. Ease in to the wall. Flattens out a bit, enough for me to plant my feet. Reach out, grab the drainpipe, test it. Nice and solid. Pull myself up to standing, feet on the stone.

And now up again, clinging to the pipe. Feels cold and wet, bit slippery. But it's still firm and that's all I care about. Up, up, taking it steady. I'm getting tired now, Bigeyes. You better believe it. But I'm holding on, somehow.

And moving up.

Voices far below. Seem like they're from another world. I twist my head, check down. Can't see a thing. All's dark down there and bunged up with mist. Another lucky break. On, on, breathing hard.

Voices still talking. I catch 'em, but not the words. Just the tone. And I think I'm cute. If someone had spotted me, they'd be talking different. Just hope I'm right. Here's the top of the roof.

Shit.

It slants down at me before it flattens out. I didn't clap that from below. And I can't see anything on it to hold. I clutch the end of the drainpipe, check round. Gutter running left and right.

Nothing else in front of me.

Just a slanty, slippery roof.

And beyond that, Hawk's tower rising.

Nothing else for it. Got to go for the roof and hope I don't slip. I pull myself up, feeling for the brackets that hold the pipe to the wall. Gutter's too weak to trust. Up, up, panting.

Half over the edge now, hands down by my waist, clinging to the top of the pipe. I don't dare take 'em off but I know I must. Crab round with my right foot, feel for the highest bracket I can hit.

Got one.

Dig the toe in, push up, grub round with my left foot. Next bracket—got it. Ease a bit higher, but now the brackets have run out and there's only the roof and whatever I can smack on it.

Cos now I got to take my hands off the pipe.

Do it.

Just do it.

I let go, feel my balance start to flip, wave my arms to get it back. Shit, Bigeyes. I'm standing on the brackets, holding nothing. Lean forward, plunge onto the roof, scrabble with my hands for something to hold.

It's almost completely smooth. Tiny grooves between the tiles and that's it. But maybe enough to grip. Got to go for it anyway. I keep my left foot on the bracket, push off with the right, plant it on the bottom tile. It slips off, catches the gutter.

'Ah!'

But the gutter holds firm. Scrape my hands over the tiles, push with my right foot, lunge with my left, and suddenly I'm scrambling up, up, up towards the top.

I don't know how it happened. I'm too scared to remember. But somehow I'm there. I'm sprawled on the flat part of the roof, gasping.

I don't move. I can't move. Not yet. In a moment but not yet. I just stay there, breathing. Waiting for the panic to drain away. Then I roll onto my back.

And see Hawk's tower rising.

And now we got the worst part of all.

Cos this crusher's got no drainpipe, no gargoyle to hook a rope onto. Just brick. And I got to climb it. But there's one good thing, Bigeyes. And I'm glad my memory hasn't let me down. Cos there's something I remembered from the past.

The bricks are chunky bastards, see? The tower wasn't part of the original building. Like I told you, Hawk had it built special. And he obviously liked these bricks.

Well, so do I, Bigeyes. Cos they're climbable.

I think.

Back on my feet, over the roof to the tower, check round. Just a dusky view of what's below. Glimpses of the ground, no more, like little windows have opened up in the mist and dark and I can see through.

But even where I got glimpses I can't see much.

So I don't reckon they can either.

Lights moving here and there, grinks flashing torches round the house, up on the slopes, over where the trees are. Pretty sure they can't see me up here, even on the tower. I reach out, touch the wall.

Feels cold and damp. Run my fingers along the grooves between the bricks. Better than the tiles but still not much to hold on to, and it's going to be worse with what I'm carrying. But there's nothing else for it.

Take off the rope, drop it on the roof. No good to me now. Done its bit. Check pockets, check the kit. Everything in place. Start to climb.

Slow, real slow, one hand up, other hand up, one foot, other foot. Inch by inch, that's how it's got to be. Least the brickwork's even. Means I know what's coming next. But the holds are narrower than I thought and the bricks are getting damper the higher I go.

Stop, take a breath. I feel so vulnerable, Bigeyes, so scared. I make myself climb on. Up, up, one brick, one victory, another brick, another victory, and on, on, closer to the top.

I know the bit I'm aiming for. It's the one part I'm certain about.

The only way in I can think of.

Where I got a chance of not being found out.

Stop again, take another breath, climb on. And here it is, Bigeyes. See? Little tiny window, just under the top of the tower. There's another one on the other side. Takes you into the bathroom. This one takes us into a storeroom.

And there's a bigger window on the very top of the tower.

A massive one.

But we're not going in that way. You'll soon find out why.

Another breath, a long one. This is the next tough part, Bigeyes. I got to force the window without falling off the wall and without being heard from inside. And here's the gripe—I got no idea if Hawk's in there or not.

All I know is what I can see from here. No light inside the storeroom and no glow under the door to the main room. He could be in there. Could be sleeping. But he shouldn't be at this time. It's not late enough.

So I'm hoping he's somewhere else. But I still don't know for certain. That's the gripe, Bigeyes. He might be at his desk with just a lamp on. And that wouldn't show under the storeroom door.

I brace myself, make sure I got both feet firm on the bricks, both hands tight in the grooves. Ease myself up, just a bit more. Check over the window. Not what you'd call big, is it? But it's enough for me.

Reach out, grab hold of the sill. Check the frame, check the catch inside. Cute little thing but nothing Ezi's burglary tools won't slam. I fix my feet again, make sure they're firm, ease my right hand off the sill, reach into my pocket, pull out Ezi's goodies.

Two minutes later I'm in.

28

CHECK ROUND, SLOW. All's dark, all's quiet. Listen cute. No sound of movement beyond the door. Flick a glance at it. Still no light underneath. Nothing I can see anyway. Look round.

Nothing much in the storeroom. Boots, heavy weather gear. Like I told you, he doesn't use this house much, so he doesn't keep a lot here. Creep up to the door. It never had a lock in the old days.

Still hasn't. Good. And it's not clicked shut either. Even better. Put an ear to it.

Nothing.

Just my breath stealing in, stealing out. I wait a moment, quieten down a bit more. Check the kit over. Check it again. And again. Everything's fine. Everything's plum.

If he's in there, if it's got to be now, I'm ready.

Reach out, stroke the door handle, hold it steady. Ease the door open, just a fraction. Darkness in the gap, then a glimpse of the nearest wall. And the familiar shapes all along it.

Hawks.

Peering down with their dead eyes.

He shot 'em all, Bigeyes. Every one. And he's got more on the other walls. Only hawks in this place. There's different stuff in his other homes. Oh, yeah, you bet. Bear skins, tiger skins, elephant tusks, rhino horns, whatever.

Like I told you, he's an expert shot.

And he loves killing.

He'll have guns up here. We won't see 'em but they'll be here. He's never far from a gun. Ease the door a little further.

More of the wall, more hawks peering down, dark like before. Push the door wider. Glint of glass up above, but I'm not looking at that. I'm checking round into the room.

No sign of the bastard. And not a light on anywhere.

Just the shadows of things I remember so well. And yeah, Bigeyes, I do remember 'em well. I was the only other person ever allowed in here. Cos I was his favourite. And he never had any other. He told me that. And I believed him.

I still believe him.

Never mind why. I just do. And that's why he wants me so bad. Wants me dead, I mean. Cos I'm still his favourite. Yeah, Bigeyes, I still am. Don't ask me how I know. So he wants me dead.

Cos I betrayed him.

I stare out over the shadowy room. The long, wide bed, beautifully made, sheets, pillows, duvet just so. Scent of flowers. Everything neat and special. He'll have done all that himself. Oh yeah. Like he'll have cleaned and dusted the room himself. Cos he always does that in his secret nest. Cos it's like I say.

There's nobody else allowed in here.

And there never has been.

Except me.

I let my eyes move on. The books on the shelves, the ornaments, the pictures, the cabinet with the hunting knives. More dead hawks looking down from the walls. The built-in wardrobes, the door into the bathroom. The desk with the anglepoise, the phone, the ugly stone paperweight.

And then the real reason why he had this tower built.

Check right, Bigeyes. And then look up.

The raised floor, the telescope, the big glass dome above. Yeah, Bigeyes. He comes up here to watch the stars. To sleep under 'em, dream under 'em. And I used to suffer under 'em.

Look up at the sky.

No stars tonight. Just mist and dark. But they're up there, Bigeyes. I know they are. I used to gaze up at 'em when I was here. In other places, I used to close my eyes when he whammed me. If I thought he couldn't see.

But not here.

I used to peer up, through the glass, used to spin my eyes over the night sky, searching for 'em, so I could forget what was happening. And sometimes it worked. When I could see 'em. I wish I could tonight.

Look down again, check over the kit.

Got to stop doing that.

It's all ready. I know it is. I just need my enemy now.

Back to the storeroom, slip in, ease the door almost closed, just a tiny gap. Slump down on the floor, back against the wall, clench my fists, let 'em go. This is the bad time. The waiting time.

Stare round.

I got Becky in my head again. But I guess that's a dimpy thing to say. I mean, think about it, Bigeyes. When's she not in my head? And I wouldn't want it any different.

I got Jaz in there too. Little poppet. And Mary. Beautiful old Mary.

'I love you guys.'

My voice sounds strange in the storeroom. Just a whisper but it's like the words spoke by themselves, out of the darkness.

'I love you guys.'

Silence again. I'm thinking of Poppa now. And Bannerman and Fern. And Ruby and her mates. And Bex. Jesus, Bigeyes, what happened to 'em all? I'm hoping like hell none of 'em got shunted when Jakes stuffed me.

But I can't help 'em now.

I can only do this. Just hope it's enough.

Do something better, Ruby said. Don't jump off a bridge. Do something better. For Becky. Yeah, Rubes, I know. But Hawk's hurt me so bad. You got to understand that. There's some things you never come back from, some things you never forgive.

Do something better. I'll try.

'For you, Becky.'

The words whisper out of the darkness again.

'For you, sweetheart.'

Footsteps climbing slow. I stiffen, stand up, check over the kit again. Lean close to the storeroom door, listen. Footsteps grow louder. A pause. Sound of a key turning, door of the main room opening.

Silence again.

A long silence. Like he's waiting, checking, making sure.

Door closes, key turns to lock it, footsteps start again. Crossing the floor, towards the bed, round the bed, stop. I keep back, away from the gap. He can't see me, I can't see him. But I'm sensing what he's doing.

He's standing still. And I can feel him looking round.

29

A LIGHT FLICKS on. Not the main light. I can tell. It's the anglepoise. Sound of a chair moving. He's sitting down at the desk. Opens a drawer, closes it, pushes back the chair. Footsteps cut off towards the bathroom.

Running water.

Not a bath or shower. He's filling a basin. I go on listening. I could move now. What's to wait for? It's a done deal. He's on his own. He's even locked the door to the room. All I got to do is get myself between him and the way out.

And make sure I plug him before he whips out one of his guns.

Piece of piss.

But I don't move.

Except my hands. They're moving, trembling. Yeah, Bigeyes. Can't stop 'em. Arms trembling too now, and my legs, shaking like I can't stop 'em. I got to get on with this.

Got to do it quick or he'll hear me, or sense me, and then he'll come for me.

I can still nail him if he does.

But I won't have surprise on my side.

And I need that.

To do this right.

But I still can't shift. And now he's moving again. Footsteps like before, out of the bathroom, back into the main room. Wardrobe door opening, hangers sliding. He's changing clothes. Could be going out again.

Too early for bed. Another reason why I got to get out there. But I still can't move. I just go on trembling, listening, aching. Then the light goes off. And the footsteps start again.

Coming this way.

I reach into my pocket, feel for what I want. It's all there, still ready. Just me that's not ready. Got to make myself, Bigeyes. I've come this far. I can't fail now. It's simple. It's so simple.

Everything I need's in this pocket. All I got to find now is a tiny act of courage to go with it. That's all. One tiny act of courage. And it's done. Cos now he's coming.

Step, step, step.

Heading straight to me. Maybe he knows I'm here, maybe he doesn't. Who gives two bells? I feel my hand relax inside the pocket. Feel the rest of me relax too. I'm OK now, Bigeyes. I'm ready. And here he is.

Step, step, step.

Coming into the storeroom.

But I'm wrong. He's stopped by the door. And it hasn't opened. He's just standing there. Maybe he's listening for me. But I'm wrong again. Cos there's another sound. Steps moving right. And now I got it.

He's walking round the inside of the tower.

And I can crack why. He's checking up, through the glass dome. Seen something in the sky, I'm guessing. And now—yeah. He's making his way up onto the raised floor.

This is it, Bigeyes.

There won't be a better time.

Ease open the door, just a bit, peer round. There he is, like I said, up on the raised floor, gazing up at the sky through the telescope. Wearing a dressing gown. Not aware of me at all. Just the sky. And I don't blame him. Cos look, Bigeyes. Mist's cleared.

And there's stars up there.

Beautiful, beautiful stars.

And a soft, sweet moon.

I take my eyes off 'em, fix Hawk again. He goes on watching the sky. Quick glance round the room. All's as it was. Bed tidy, desk tidy. Clothes put away out of sight. Just him and me. And an empty room.

I slip round the door, walk softly over to the bed, stop, my eyes on Hawk. He's still gazing into the telescope, his back to me. Then suddenly he stiffens, straightens, turns.

And smiles down at me.

I stiffen too. Can't help myself. I keep my face still. Just fix him back, hard as I can. He goes on smiling. Looks relaxed, calm, happy to see me. Like we're old mates. Like it's been too long. Like I should have got in touch.

I go on watching. And not just his face. I'm checking his hands. Pretty sure he's got nothing on under that dressing gown, but it's got two pockets, and like I said—he's never far from a gun.

I keep my hand in my own pocket.

Cos that's the key.

The thing that's in there. That's what nails him. I move my hand round it, squeeze gentle. Ready to go. He can't beat me on this, Bigeyes. I take a step closer. Don't need to. I could stand back by the door and still plug him.

But I want to see his face.

And I want him to see mine.

See it good.

But I go on watching his hands.

He's still smiling, like nothing's wrong. Then slowly he starts to move, down to the right, off the raised floor, past the storeroom, back towards the desk, walking casual, soft eyes watching me.

He doesn't come close.

Just saunters past, well out of reach.

Heading for the desk.

I speak.

'Stop.'

He does. Looks me over. The smiles fades.

'Was that an order?' he says.

The smile comes back.

'Because I don't take orders.'

And he walks on towards the desk. I feel my hand twitch in my pocket. Doesn't matter, all this. He can mock, play games. He was always going to do that. I'm still in control. There's no gun on that desk. Probably is in one of the drawers. Or all of 'em.

But he's not close enough yet. And now he's stopped. By himself.

Still smiling at me. I go on watching his hands. They're hovering over his pockets. The smile fades again and I see the face that's haunted me for three years. The face that's never loved. And now never will.

He moves his hands. Still calm, relaxed, like there's no hurry. Reaches into his pockets, turns 'em out, shows me they're empty, takes a step back, sits on the edge of the desk.

Watching me.

I stare back at him. It's like he hasn't aged at all. He's just grown younger, stronger, more beautiful. I hate him so much. He speaks.

'So am I the target this time?'

30

I DON'T ANSWER. Hawk raises an eyebrow.

'You can't win, you know.'

Somewhere far away I hear the drone of an engine. More than one engine. Hawk catches it too, gives a chuckle.

'More reinforcements. You can never have too many. Especially when there are dangerous killers on the loose.' He looks me over. 'Not that you're really dangerous. To be honest, I find you rather pathetic. I mean, you don't really think you can kill me, do you?'

'You're already dead,' I murmur.

Again he raises an eyebrow. The sound of the engines goes on. Still distant, but getting louder. I don't bother about 'em. Whatever they are, they can't save this bastard. And that's all I care about.

'So what's in the pocket?' he goes on. 'A knife, I suppose.'

I keep my hand in there. Tight, ready.

'Not a knife,' I say. 'Given up on knives.'

'A gun, then.'

I shake my head.

'Too risky. I might miss with a gun.'

Hawk's face darkens. For the first time.

And something passes over his eyes. Something I've never seen before. A shiver of fear. His gaze moves back to my hand, my pocket. I keep watching his face. Cos he could spring any moment.

The sound of the engines grows louder. Christ knows how many motors he's got rolling in. Bloody convoy, I reckon. But all the backup in the world won't save him now. Cos it's just him and me in here. And that's all I ever wanted.

'What's in the pocket, Blade?' he says.

'A detonator switch.'

I pause, watch, speak again.

'I'm wearing a bomb vest.'

I unzip the coat with my free hand, let him see underneath. He doesn't move, just stares. Sound of car doors slamming, footsteps on the gravel. I nod upwards, towards the glass dome.

'Get ready, Hawk. Cos we're going to the stars together. In pieces.'

I brace myself, start to squeeze the switch—then freeze. Cos suddenly there's a new sound. A small, soft sound. It checks me, fills me with terror. Cos it's not from down below.

It's from inside this room.

Gone quiet again. But I heard it. I know I did. Somewhere near the bed. A small, creeping movement. But it can't be. I checked the room. And I can't check again. Can't take my eyes off Hawk.

Not for one second.

I keep my hand on the detonator switch. It's still half-pressed and me and Hawk are halfway into death. But who else is too? And does it matter? Cos if it's some grink in the room, he can come with us. But what if I'm wrong?

What if it's someone else?

I see the change in Hawk's face.

See the confidence come back.

The smile.

Then catch the sound again. A small, stealthy movement, somewhere to the left. I flick my head round. Can't help it. I know I shouldn't. But I got to know. Whip a glance over the end of the room.

Nothing.

Same as before.

Nobody on the bed, nobody in it, nobody this side of it. But I can't see the other side. Can't see if there's someone creeping along the floor. And I don't get the chance. Cos even as I snap back to watch Hawk, something hard smashes into my face.

I stagger, head spinning. Somehow I stay on my feet. Through a blur I see Hawk bent over the desk. He must have flung the paperweight and now he's digging in a drawer.

I fumble with my right hand. It jerked out of my pocket when I got hit, darted up to cover my face.

Couldn't stop it. I try to squeeze it back into the pocket with the detonator.

Crack!

A bullet rips up my wrist. I give a yelp of pain.

Crack!

Another bullet, upper arm.

More pain and now blood's starting to gush. I'm swinging my arm, trying to shove my hand back in the pocket, but it won't go. And here's Hawk striding forward.

Crack!

Third bullet. Ploughs into my thigh.

I go down, hard on my back. The floor thumps the breath out of me. I'm bleeding bad now, fighting blacko, but I keep trying to ram my hand into the pocket. Hawk dives on top of me, pins my right arm back, thrusts the shooter under my coat, feels round the bomb vest till he finds a spot on my body.

Digs the gun-point into me, leans close, hisses.

'Stupid. So stupid.'

His eyes cut into mine.

'Did you really think you could kill me?'

His breath's hot. Yeah, Bigeyes. Hot. It always was. I remember. He shoves the gun-point harder against me.

'Really thought you were special, didn't you?'

I don't answer. I can't. I got blood filling my mouth, filling my eyes. He gives a low, animal laugh.

'You were never special,' he growls. 'I'll tell you what you were. You were just another boy off the street. Just another worthless piece of trash. Because that's what you all are. Every single one of you. Worthless trash.'

His mouth curls into a sneer.

'I can't wait to see you die.'

He eases back, just a bit, the gun still hard against me. I know what he's doing. He wants to see better. Wants to watch me twitch, bleed, flicker, go still. I don't care, Bigeyes. He can watch what he likes now.

There's nothing I can do to stop him.

I just wish I hadn't failed. Cos I should have killed him. For Becky's sake.

He smiles that smile. The one I know so well.

'Goodbye, Blade,' he whispers.

He skews the tip of the gun towards my heart, then suddenly rears up, the smile twisted off him. I stare up, confused, and see horror in his eyes. He gives a gasp, then falls over me, spluttering.

I stare past his shoulder and see a small boy standing there.

About seven years old, naked. He's got whip-slashes all over his body. And he's holding one of Hawk's hunting knives. It's got blood on it.

Hawk stirs. He's breathing hard, jerky. The boy got him in the lower back but it hasn't killed him. I look up at the kid. He's so like me, Bigeyes. Same face, same eyes, same fear. Yeah, specially that.

I mutter to him.

'Get out of here, boy. Find your clothes and run. Just . . . run.'

Sound of voices outside the room. Gobbos calling out. I'm guessing they heard the shots. Someone bangs the door. I reach down with my left hand, feel for the gun. Got to prise it away before Hawk recovers.

But it's too late.

He's picked up the movement. He gives a moan, whips the gun away from me, thrusts it back under my coat, stabs it against my body. More shouts from outside, more thumping on the door. Getting louder and louder, and now the pain's tearing me apart.

I fix the boy's eyes.

He's all that matters now.

'Run for it,' I mumble. 'Just . . . just . . . '

I hear Hawk snarl, feel him steady the gun.

Then everything goes black.

31

AND STAYS THAT way. Doesn't change. Just goes on. An endless black. But I know where I am. Oh, you bet. I recognize this place. I've been here before. It's lonely but it's cool. Just black silence and me.

Or what's left of me. Cos I'm zippo now. A mind moving through nothing. Searching for a way to die. Yeah, that's right. I'm looking for him.

Death.

Scummy bastard.

I met him once, remember? Just after Dig cut my head. Met him close, face to face. He played games with me, spun my brain, put me in his bag, zipped it up—then let me out again.

And I lived.

Bastard.

What's he going to do this time? When he fixes me with his eyes. Cos he's not far away. Don't ask me how I know. I can feel his soft sad breath whispering over me. But I'm cute about that.

I want to die so much.

I can't wait to see him.

But now there's other faces turning up instead. I don't want to see 'em. I want to see Death's face. He's the only gobbo I'm after. But these other ones are crowding round.

'Get lost,' I murmur.

I scowl at 'em, try to brush 'em away. They don't go. They bustle round. Dark, scary faces. And now I recognize 'em. It's the dronks I killed. Every one. They're moving round me, staring, just staring.

Jesus, Bigeyes.

Is that what Death's got waiting for me? The dregs I plugged with my knife? Is that how you pay back what you owe? You kill these dungpots and then get stuck with 'em for eternity?

They go on moving round me.

Then I catch a voice.

'Blade.'

I wish it was Mary. I remember when she called my name. That time I was blacko and she brought me out. With that sweet Irish voice. But it's not Mary. It's some gobbo.

'Blade.'

I wish he'd shut up. I'm trying to die here.

And I can't with him blabbing.

'Blade,' he goes.

'Piss off.'

He doesn't piss off. Just goes on saying my name.

'Shut your mouth,' I grumble.

I stare at the faces. Still moving round me, but they're further back than they were. I fix 'em. They're all watching me. And here's something I don't get. They don't look angry. Why not?

They should be steaming at me.

Cos I plugged 'em all.

Yeah, yeah, they were scum. They probably still are scum. Me killing 'em won't have changed that. So why aren't they ripping off at me? Why don't they hate me?

They should. Cos I hate me.

Oh, yeah. I hate me.

'Blade,' says the voice again.

The faces disappear. And it's just blackness again. Only I'm wrong. There's one face left. Can't see it clear. It's kind of hovering over me. And now I'm seeing something else. This face—it's not one of those scumbos.

It's some other face. A face that wasn't there before. Still hard to see in all this black. And now there's another thing I'm getting. It's not just hard to see cos of the black. The face itself is black.

'Blade,' it says.

A low, slow voice.

'Come back to us, boy.'

I'm not coming back. I'm bloody staying here. And hanging round till I hook up with Death. He's got to get here soon. I just got to keep looking for him. The black gobbo's face has faded. Thank God for that. But now he's started talking again.

'You got to fight this, boy. You hear me? Biggest fight you ever had. Cos you hurt bad. You hurt real bad. So come on. Give us what you got.'

I'm not giving him anything. I'm staying put.

And when Death turns up, I'm diving straight in his bag. Wigging it out of here. All the way to nothing. Beautiful, beautiful nothing. You know why, Bigeyes? Cos I failed. Failed bad.

Didn't avenge Becky. Didn't kill Hawk.

And that little kid won't have done either. A knife dink in the back won't have nailed it. Hawk'll have turned round after shooting me and blown the kid's head off. I just wish he'd blown mine off too. I'd have been dead quicker.

But I'm almost there.

Just need a bit of quiet.

And I'll be gone.

But here's that gobbo's voice again. And now there's something strange. It sounds familiar. Why's that? Didn't sound familiar before. And I didn't recognize the face when I had it. Maybe it was too blurred. I just knew it wasn't one of the slugs I killed.

'Come on, boy,' says the voice. 'Don't give up.'

Yeah, I got it now. Who the guy is, I mean.

But he tells me anyway.

'It's Poppa,' he says. 'Becky's grandpa.'

Wish he hadn't said that. The last bit. He didn't need to. Just makes it worse. Hearing her name. Makes me want to die even more. It's not Poppa's fault, bless his heart. How's he to know how bad I failed? How I can't bear to face him? Or Becky's mum.

And Ruby's bound to be here with him.

I'm dreading hearing her voice.

But it's still Poppa doing the talking. Only something's changed suddenly. He's not speaking to me. He's speaking to someone else, and he's talking quick. And Poppa never talks quick.

'Doctor!' he's saying. 'He's going!'

Footsteps, another voice.

'Nurse, over here!'

And suddenly there's gabbling all around.

'We're losing him,' someone says.

I take no notice. Cos you know what? Suddenly the black's got deeper—and oh, you beauty, you're squeezing me away, squeezing out everything Blade ever was, and now he's gone and there's just this tiny little bit left.

A flickering spark of what I might have been. Too late to mend, too late to start again. And now that's going too. Thank Christ. Cos here's the gobbo I've been looking for. I knew he'd come. I knew he wouldn't let me down.

Death.

Sweet lovely Death. Come to take me away.

Yeah, big man. Close me up, pop me in your little bag. Let's go.

But we don't go. Cos suddenly there's words again. Only they're not like normal words. They're floating in the darkness like a frozen dream.

'Don't die for Becky.'

I feel a shudder. Cos it's not Death talking. It's another voice. A voice I'm even more scared of. There's a long silence. A long, black silence. Then Ruby speaks again.

'Live for Becky,' she says.

32

SO I LIVE. But it's a strange, dusky life. Cos everything's shadows right now. I'm not speaking. Can't speak. Don't know why. I want to. I want to say lots. I want to find out what happened.

But every time I open my mouth, nothing comes.

So I listen to everybody else.

And there's plenty of nebs to fizz onto. They're all naffing. Yak yak yak, all around me. Can't see 'em clear. Like I say, they're all shadows. And I can't hear 'em good either. Not the words, I mean. Just the yakky drone.

They're hospital nebs. I worked that out. But not much else. Except that I like 'em. Yeah, they're cool. They keep checking me over. One of 'em stroked my face, made a cooing noise. Felt good. And one time they rushed round, bustling. I can't remember what was wrong.

Something to do with me.

Cos I went blacko again.

But it wasn't scary. Not this time. I saw Becky's face in there. And it felt good. And somehow I knew Ruby was right. I knew I was going to come back. Eventually. And I did. I woke up. And the hand stroked my face again.

And so it's gone on. They've moved me a couple of times. Maybe more times than I know. Cos I keep sleeping. Can't stay awake, except when the pain kicks in. And someone rushes over. And it goes dark again.

But here's the thing, Bigeyes. I've kind of stopped worrying. I want to live for Becky. I've decided that. But you know what? If I don't make it, that's cool too. Cos then I'll get to meet her.

And how good would that be?

So now it's simple. Win and live, win and die.

Yeah, yeah. I know what you're thinking. You're thinking—win? Who's won what? Cos we still don't know what happened to Hawk. That's true, Bigeyes. Good point. But I'll tell you something. Something I worked out in this dreamy little world I'm in.

There's winning and there's winning.

And I know one thing. Whatever else I've done wrong, I've done one or two things right. And you know what? I'm going to call that winning. Winning something back. Something I can give to Becky.

And make her forgive me.

Maybe even love me.

I've been thinking about that a lot. Love, I mean. Cos the thing is, I never dreamt Becky could possibly love me.

That time I told you what I saw in her face, and Mary's face, and Jaz's face—remember what I called it?

The opposite of hate.

The thing that couldn't be love.

But why couldn't it be love? Eh? Cos here's something that's slammed me. Last time I saw Becky's face, when I was blacko, she wasn't like in that photo of Ruby's. Or even like in my memory. Cos in those pictures she's kind of a goddess. I look at her and think—how could she possibly love a claphead like me?

How could anyone?

But when I was blacko, she didn't look like that. She just looked at me like . . . like it's OK, like I'm OK, like I'm still her friend. Like . . . she maybe could love me.

Like she maybe always did.

The hand's stroking my face again. I try to look, try to see who it is. But it's just a shadow. A friendly shadow. Murmurs something. I go on thinking about Becky. The hand rests on my cheek, moves away.

And Becky stays. Warm in my heart.

More dreams, more pain. Time's gone somewhere. Wigged it. I don't know where. Got no idea how long I've been here. Or where I am. Yeah, yeah, some hospital. That's bung-clear. But don't ask me where it is.

I got a feeling I've been here several days. But I don't give two bells. Cos days have stopped being days now and it's like I'm floating through an endless night. Then suddenly it clears. I open my eyes and I don't see the dark.

I see sunlight pouring in through a window. I see a room with pale walls, artificial flowers, screens round part of the bed. Bleepy hospital gizmos. Shit painting on the far wall.

And Bex, sitting in a chair.

Watching my face.

I twist my head. It does what I want. Didn't expect it to. But it moves good. Cop a glint round. No other beds and nobody here. Just me and Bex. Sound of nursey voices down the corridor. I turn my head back, look at Bex.

She stands up, comes over, leans down.

'Can you see me?' she says.

Her voice is strange. The words sound clipped, like they never were with Bex. But maybe it's just me. I haven't heard proper words for a bit. She speaks again. And her voice sounds like it used to.

'Blade? Can you see me?'

'Yeah.'

'Jesus, you can talk!'

'Course I can bloody talk.'

'I'll go and get the others.'

'Wait.'

I try to reach out. But my arm feels heavy. She stays anyway.

'Take it easy,' she says.

'I'm all right.'

'You look like shit.'

'Piss off.'

She glances towards the corridor. I can tell she's thinking she's got to get help. Case I'm not right.

'I'm OK, Bex.'

'What?'

She's leaning close to hear. And I realize she's right. I must look like shit. Cos I still feel like shit. And just speaking those few words has worn me out. I'm probably talking softer than I thought.

I take a slow breath.

'Bex?'

'Yeah?'

'Before . . . before you get anybody . . . tell me what happened.'

She flicks another glance towards the corridor, then pulls her chair close, sits down, leans in.

'Can you hear me all right?' she says.

'Yeah, but . . . don't speak too fast.'

She talks slow.

'I don't know much, OK? About what happened. Police won't tell us. Just know my dad's been arrested. That's it. And you nearly died Christ knows how many times. You got shot to pieces. You know that, don't you? Doc says either you fought hard or you got lucky. Or it's just a miracle.'

I'll settle for the miracle, Bigeyes.

She leans closer.

'Ain't got much more to tell you. I ran away from my dad. And my bitch stepmother. Headed for Ruby's place. Found her there with a load of her mates. Big guy called

Seth, three women, couple of other guys. You probably remember 'em. She said you was with 'em.'

'I remember. But what happened to 'em? I got . . . '

I feel the pain come back, and the weariness.

'Do you want to stop?' says Bex.

'No, listen . . . ' I take another long breath. 'I got taken away, OK? By your dad's men.'

'I know about that bit. Ruby told me. She saw it out of the window of her house. My dad's a bastard. What did he do to you?'

'Never mind that. I got to know what happened to you? And Ruby and her mates?'

'Nothing. They was all OK. There was a bit of trouble with them guys what come looking for you. They roughed up Seth a bit. Threatened Ruby and the others. But nothing more. They all pissed off after you got took away.'

So it was that simple, Bigeyes. Jakes set the trap and it was just for me. Thank Christ for that. Nobody else got shunted. And Bex is OK. I think. I look at her.

'Where you living now?'

'With Ruby.'

I relax. She'll be OK with Ruby. Ruby'll take care of her. Till Bex moves on. Which she will. Cos she always will. She's that kind of troll. Don't ask me how I know.

Bex hesitates.

'Ruby told me about Jaz. What you done for her.'

She leans forward suddenly, kisses me on the cheek. Stands up quick.

'I'm getting the others,' she mutters.

But they're coming in anyway. Couple of nurses, a gobbo. I can tell he's the doc. Looks kind of young, but I like his face. And there's two more nebs. I feel a shiver run through me. A dronky kind of shiver.

Cos I'm happy and scared at the same time.

Ruby and Poppa.

They're standing back, letting the medics fiddle round. Nurses doing most of the fiddling, naffing at me quiet and friendly. How do they do that? Make like they're just talking to you casual but what they're really doing is checking you over.

The gobbo's doing his bit now. And he's naffing too. Talking to me like they are, the kind of talk that doesn't need an answer. And that's just as well cos I got nothing in me to answer anybody. Not right now.

That little bit of talking with Bex wiped me out.

'You don't need to answer,' says the doc.

Yeah, mate. Like I haven't worked that out.

They go on fiddling, checking pulse, blood pressure, whatever. Taking ages, and all the time I'm watching Ruby and Poppa. They're standing back, keeping out of the way, saying nothing. Just watching me.

Watching them.

Bex has sat down, but they're still standing. One of the nurses has pulled up a couple of free chairs for 'em, but they don't take 'em. They just stand there and watch. And I watch back. And it's like I said, Bigeyes.

I feel happy and scared seeing 'em.

Scared cos of the guilt. Yeah, I know. I probably shouldn't feel choked out. I mean, look at their faces. There's nothing in 'em that wants me to be frightened. Poppa looks just like he did the last time.

Old and sad and kind.

And Ruby?

Ruby looks . . .

Never mind. I guess I'm still scared of Ruby.

The doc's talking again, and this time he wants an answer.

'OK.' He looks hard at me. 'You can talk to your friends for just a few minutes. But I mean just a few. One of the nurses will come back and tell you when to stop. All right?'

I manage something with my eyes.

And he picks it up.

'Good.' He straightens up. 'We'll leave you to it. But take it easy. You'll find talking more tiring than you think.'

He looks round the room. And I can tell he's waiting for another answer. Ruby gives him a nod. And he picks that up too. A glance at the nurses and the medics wig it out the room.

Poppa and Ruby walk slowly up to the bed. Bex stands up and joins 'em. They stand there close by, all three of 'em, looking down at me. Then Poppa leans close, takes my hand, squeezes it gentle, speaks to me in that soft, slow voice.

'So have you stopped running now, son?'

I look up at him.

'Yeah, Poppa. I stopped running now.'

He's got tears in his eyes. Doesn't say any more. Just squeezes my hand again. I look up at Ruby. I so want her to speak. I want her to say something. Anything. Long as I can take it. But she doesn't speak. She just reaches out.

Rests a hand on my cheek.

I close my eyes. Cos suddenly I recognize that hand. It's the hand I felt before. When everything was dark. It wasn't one of the nurses. It was Ruby. Touching my face, murmuring. It was Ruby. Or maybe . . .

Maybe it was someone else.

I almost dare to think so.

33

SO WHAT DO you know? Here we are again. Back at the old police station. Same room even. The one they shoved me in when I was seven and got jacked for stopping cars on the pedestrian crossing and swearing at the drivers.

Jesus, that was a gig.

Yeah, same old room. They might have done it up. But they've changed it a bit. The desk's different. And they got video kit in here for the interview. They didn't have that last time. Otherwise it's the same.

Apart from me being stuck in a wheelchair.

And getting blobbed with this gobbo from Social Services. They keep telling me I got to have him. For legal reasons. Can't be interviewed without him present. They say. I got nothing against him personal. I just don't need him.

I know how this works. I've been arrested and cautioned. I'm up for multiple murders. Now I'm going to get grilled. And I'm cute about that. I'm ready for what comes.

Apart from the journos outside. Wasn't quite ready for them. Or that many of 'em. I kind of forgot I'm big news. But never mind that. One thing at a time. Check round the room again.

Soggy Service guy's standing in the corner and there's a porker woman behind me. She's been pushing my wheelchair. Then there's the two porkers who came and got me from the hospital. Gloomy-looking gobbos.

Door opens and in comes DI Fern.

She's followed by Inspector Bannerman.

Jesus, Bigeyes. I wasn't expecting these two. Not him anyway.

They sit down behind the desk, fiddle with papers, keep their eyes away from mine. Bannerman gives a cough, glances up at the policewoman behind my wheelchair.

'We'll take care of that,' he says. 'Just move him a bit closer to the desk so the video picks him up.'

She eases me forward.

'That's fine,' says Bannerman.

She locks the wheels, then wigs it out the room. The two porker gobbos do the same. And now it's just four of us. Soggy pulls a chair up next to mine.

I glance at him, then turn to Bannerman.

'I don't need this guy.'

'He's required to be present,' says Bannerman. 'It's for your own support. He's simply here to observe proceedings and ensure that—'

'I know what he's here for. I just don't need him.'

I can see I'm getting nowhere. I bung a glance at Soggy.

'Don't take this the wrong way but . . . keep your mouth shut, OK?'

The guy shrugs. Doesn't answer. And that's cute with me. Long as he keeps that way. I turn back to Bannerman and Fern. They've started the video recorder and Bannerman's muttering the date and time and all the other gobbledyplonk. He finishes that and looks me in the eye.

I give him a wink.

'Got your old job back, Bannerman.'

'So it seems.'

'Like old times, then, yeah? Me sitting here, you sitting there. And Ferny.' I glance at her. 'Only you used to stand by the door.'

'I've been promoted,' she says.

I think that was a joke. But I'm not sure. I look back at Bannerman.

'So aren't you going to check?'

'Check what?' he says.

'That I haven't got a knife in my sock.'

'I'll take the risk.'

He's watching me hard. And I'm reading something in his face. It's not in Fern's, but it's in his. He's going through the procedure, yeah, doing what he's got to do, but his eyes are saying, let's cut the crap. You want to know stuff, I want to know stuff. Just give me what you got and I'll do the same.

Cos I'll tell you something, Bigeyes. He's reading my face too.

Reading it good.

'OK,' I say. 'No shit. You tell me what happened to you. I'll tell you what happened to me.'

He doesn't answer. But I know what he's thinking. He's thinking, how far can I go with this kid? Cos the thing is, Bigeyes, there's limits to what he can tell me. I know that. He can't say much about Jakes, for example—if anything—cos the bastard's been arrested and there's a separate investigation going on.

And we got a video rolling and Fern sitting there all proper and official, and Soggy making sure everything's done cute. So Bannerman's got to follow the script. But he also knows he's got to tell me something. If I'm going to talk too.

'Come on, Bannerman,' I murmur. 'I know the tricks. So forget the usual crap. You tell me your bit. As much as you want. And I'll tell you my bit.' I pause. 'As much as I want.'

He raises an eyebrow. Fern looks disapproving. The video goes on rolling. I lean forward, far as I can in the wheelchair.

'Listen, Bannerman, here's the thing. I wrote those lists out for you, remember?'

'I remember.'

'Well, they weren't just to help you clean up scum. They were also my confession. For the murders I did. I gave you all the names, wrote 'em out clear. Didn't miss a single one. So you got 'em all. Every dreg I ever killed. And I'm not denying any of 'em. I'm pleading guilty to all the murders on that list.'

'And what about the other murder?' says Fern quietly. There's a silence.

'Lord Haffler-Devereaux,' says Bannerman.

I take a slow breath, lean back in the wheelchair again.

Lord Haffler-Devereaux. Yeah, Bigeyes. He died after all.

Thank Christ.

But nobody's going to tell me any more about it here. And I know why. Cos they're hoping I'm going to tell them. That's what this cosy chat's really about.

I think of that little boy. The tiny frightened kid who looked like me, could have been me. The seven-year-old me. I've been thinking about him a lot, Bigeyes. Wondering what happened to him.

And if he's still alive.

Nobody's mentioned him yet. So I won't either. I got to play this cute. I see Fern and Bannerman watching me. Waiting for what I got. I shake my head.

'You first,' I mutter. 'Then I'll talk.'

Bannerman frowns, glances at Fern, takes the plunge.

'You gave me those lists,' he says, 'and they were very helpful. But you also told me where I could find a backup hard drive from Lord Haffler-Devereaux's computer.'

He pauses, still frowning, then goes on.

'I put down the phone after speaking to you, drove through the night and dug it up.'

'But it did no good,' I cut in. 'Cos you just gave it to Jakes. And he smashed it up. I saw him do it.'

Bannerman rolls his eyes.

'Do you think I'm completely stupid?'

'Only sometimes.'

'I drove to DI Fern's on the way back. She copied all the material and I handed in the drive to my superior in the morning, together with the lists you gave me. I took copies of those too and gave them to DI Fern. During the day when I was suspended, DI Fern went through the computer files.'

OK, Bigeyes, I got it. And I'm starting to see the whole thing. Bannerman played it good, no question. Covered himself so even when Jakes blasted him, he could kick back. What I don't get is why it took Fern so long to smack the files on that backup drive.

The whole of the next day at least.

Cos that was the day I got caught and beaten up. If she'd splashed the stuff out quicker, Jakes might have got taken sooner and I might never have got snagged. But I guess I was meant to. Cos otherwise I might never have gone after Hawk.

Even so . . .

I look at Fern. She's still got that official face. I won't get much out of her. But I'll give it a go. She might just tell me.

'What was on the backup drive?' I go.

She presses her lips together. Yeah, OK. She's not going to tell me anything. But then suddenly she answers.

'There were hundreds and hundreds of files,' she says. 'Every imaginable type. It was just as well you gave us the passwords. But it still took me the whole day and much of the evening to go through the material. And I'd almost given up hope of finding anything. Ninety-nine per cent of the files were completely above board. But then right at the end I found the few that weren't.'

She narrows her eyes.

'And they were dynamite.'

She doesn't say any more, but she doesn't need to. I've worked out the rest. By the time she got to the end of those files, I was halfway to Hawk's nest. She probably shared what she had with someone in authority, someone she could trust.

And the porkers got cracking.

Pulled in Jakes. I'm guessing Fern found his name in one of those files. Jakes blotches on Hawk to help his own case, squeals on where the nest is. Bannerman's brought back into the fold and they all blast off.

And now I'm thinking of those last moments in Hawk's tower. When I was lying on my back and heard shouts outside the door. I'd already heard motors, remember? A convoy of 'em. And Hawk said they were backup. Well, maybe they were.

But not for him.

I'm guessing it was Bannerman and the porkers storming in.

'You found me in the tower,' I say. 'Lying there, shot, right?'

Bannerman nods. I feel Soggy shift on his chair. I glance at him. He says nothing, just watches. I think of the little boy again. Look back at Bannerman and Fern.

And start to talk.

I tell 'em what happened. Or most of what happened. Trying to jump off Bogeybum Bridge, Ruby rescuing me, taking me back to Poppa's, getting caught by Jakes, handed over to Hawk's grinks.

Getting beaten up, getting away.

Picking up the bomb vest. I don't say who from.

And they don't ask.

The video goes on rolling.

I tell 'em about driving to Hawk's nest, watching the house, climbing up the wall, breaking in to the tower. Hawk coming in, watching the stars. Turning to face me. And then I stop.

Cos I can't tell 'em more. Without them telling me more.

The silence feels heavy, strained. Bannerman speaks suddenly.

'There's something that's not right,' he says.

'What's that?'

He looks at me.

'You went in there, risking all, strapped inside a bomb vest. We're not here to question your motivation for suicide. But if murder was your other intention, as seems to be the case, I would have thought that the bomb vest on its own would have been sufficient to kill both you and your enemy.'

Bannerman leans forward on the desk.

'So why with such a weapon at your disposal did you bother to stab Lord Haffler-Devereaux repeatedly in the back? And so very messily. The coroner noted that the stab wounds were amateurish. They weren't accurate, they weren't deep. They were just messy. It's hardly the work of a practised assassin. And how did you manage it anyway? Since he clearly had a gun and used it on you.'

I feel a shudder run through me.

Repeatedly? Stabbed repeatedly?

I think of the boy again. That tiny little kid. Did he do that? Did he really do that? I hope he got away. Trouble is, even if he did, what did he get away to? What kind of a future? I think of what I was, Bigeyes. What I've become. What I want to be. What I desperately want to be.

Something else.

Something better.

I turn my face to the video camera.

'I killed Lord Haffler-Devereaux. I did it cos of all the stuff he did to me. I was going to just blow us both up. But I couldn't help myself. He started mocking me so I whipped a knife into his back. He went down but I kept on stabbing him. I just couldn't stop, even after I thought he was dead. I hated him so much. That's why I made a mess of it. I wasn't thinking straight. But then I kind of calmed down and stopped and turned away. But he must have still been alive cos he plugged me with his gun. But I don't remember any of that. I just went unconscious.'

I look away. Can't face the video camera.

It's easier to lie to Bannerman.

But I don't think he believes me either.

'So what did you do with the knife?' he says.

I'm still looking away. Can't face any of 'em now. Not even Bannerman. All I can look at is the picture in my head of that little boy. Holding a hunting knife he never should have picked up.

'I got rid of it, Pugface,' I say.

Soggy speaks for the first time.

'Pugface?'

I look round at him.

'My pet name for Inspector Bannerman.'

I glance over at Fern.

'I got one for you too. But I don't reckon you want to hear it.'

She doesn't answer. Just asks another question.

'Are you really asking us to believe that you got rid of the knife in the brief moment between stabbing Lord Haffler-Devereaux and getting shot?'

'Yeah.'

'Don't you think that's something of an achievement?'

I look down at the floor.

'Nothing to it,' I whisper.

Yeah, Bigeyes.

Nothing to it.

34

AND ALL THAT happened when I was fourteen.

Yeah, Bigeyes. Long time ago.

Now that I've turned twenty-one, I look back and you know what's weird? It's like nothing's changed. I still don't like the police and I still don't like people getting close.

But it's not as bad as it was when I was a kid.

Cos to be honest with you, there was nobody I liked back then. Apart from sweet Becky of course. Yeah, right. I'm zipping you over. I'm not being honest. Truth is, I wasn't looking out for friends in those days. I was looking out for grime.

Cos that's all I'd ever known.

But since that time I've found lots of nebs to care for. And some of 'em even care for me. For all the crap I've done. I didn't use to believe it. But I do now. Feels kind of good. To be cared for, I mean. So I guess that's one crack up the line.

And there's another thing.

Prison's OK.

It's rough but it's OK. You got to see the shit coming and long as you do that, you got options. Blast out or blast back. Whatever works. I got a name goes with me so I'm there for the slam. And some of 'em try it.

So I got to watch cute all the time, right?

First place they put me in was for young kids. They didn't call it prison. They called it 'secure accommodation'. Yeah, right. It's a prison, OK? Good nebs running it. No claphead officers. And they treated me fair, no question.

The other kids weren't too friendly but once the crap died down about who I was and how I fitted in, things got better and it was almost like being in a snug. Better than a snug really. Cos in a snug you're always on your own. But in prison you get something else.

You get help.

I got given this counsellor gobbo called Dominic, and we talk regular, which is good, cos I like him. And I need it. Talking, I mean. To straighten me out a bit, make sense of the flashbacks and nightmares. And there's a priest called Father Brendan. I like him too. And there's nebs from Soggy Services, and mentors and stuff.

And then there's something else.

There's books.

Yeah, Bigeyes, books.

I started reading Day One. Pretty soon I'd read everything they had in the prison library so they had to get more books in for me. And then I started doing something Becky always wanted me to do.

Getting educated.

Yeah, that's right. Doing lessons. Cos they got all that bung organized in these places. You got to be up for it, but if you are, they fix you up with tutors. It's great. You can learn as much as you want. They're big time into that. You learning, I mean.

And there's one thing I learned straight up.

Well, two things.

First, Becky was right. It's fun. And second, it's a whack. I'm telling you, Bigeyes, the stuff they give kids in schools is a jink. Well, it is for me anyway. End of the first year they'd run out of things I couldn't do.

So they got me taking exams.

Whacked on through those, bang bang bang, nothing to 'em, and I get to like fifteen, sixteen years old, and I'm taking stuff they do at university. Year or two later I'm through that.

They move me on to another prison. For young offenders. Same again. Just a different name. And older kids having a pop at me. Anyway, I keep on studying. And it's just the same.

Nothing to it. They kept trying to find subjects that weren't easy piss for me. But everything was easy piss. So they gave me these intelligence tests. High level stuff, you know? The tests they give the really nerdy nobs.

And I kind of freaked everybody out with the results.

Cos I was pretty much off the scale.

That's when they started making special arrangements for me. The prison nebs, I mean. To keep me fizzing along. Can't say they haven't bent over backwards for me. Cos they have. They've been brilliant. They already had me massive into distance learning. Now they fixed up for me to see these special tutors.

You know, brainboxes.

Like the Maths guy. Clever Trevor, I call him. Yeah, I know. Not very original. Anyway, he's mega into Maths, this dronk. And I mean serious, spooky Maths. He's on another planet, reality-wise, but he's wired into Maths.

And I really hooked on with him.

Total disaster as a human being. No social skills and a voice like a farting balloon, but I don't give two bells. His lessons are a blitz. He just starts talking about numbers and every time he takes me to a new place.

And there's other tutors they brought in special.

I won't mention 'em all.

Except Dorothea. Can't leave her out. Retired professor, super bloody bright, keeps losing her pen. We started going through literature and history and philosophy and stuff. She couldn't believe I can read a book in an hour. Proper, I mean. But once I'd done a few books and shown her I got what was in 'em, we were cool.

And we still are.

She's not stuffy. Got a brain like a bee. We'll be talking about Jane Austen or Shakespeare or whatever and she'll suddenly go, 'Did you know Napoleon found it hard to sit on his horse at Waterloo because he was suffering from piles?'

So yeah, Bigeyes. Prison's OK.

Long as I watch my back.

And now they moved me to this new one. With the grown-up dronks. I guess it means I've grown up too. But you know what? Same again. I keep my nose clean, give no trouble. And on the whole I get none back.

Thing is, in prison, you got to act smart. Got to know when to talk, when to say nothing. And when you do talk, you got to say it right. It's all about respect here. If you got that, you get a quiet life.

And that's all I want now, Bigeyes.

That and books.

And the nebs I just told you about.

And the visitors.

Yeah, Bigeyes. I get visitors too.

Bannerman comes in. We get on good now. I guess we always did. He's left the porkers. Says he wants to devote more time to his drinking. I don't ever see Fern. I think they split up. If they were ever together. And here's something plum.

Jaz is doing fine. Bannerman told me last time I saw him. Said he'd made a few enquiries cos he knows I care. I had to look away, Bigeyes. I don't mind admitting it. Cos I think about Jaz a lot. Can't quite believe she'll be close on eleven.

Same age Becky was when she died.

Anyway . . .

Bex used to come in but she's kind of faded. Got a boyfriend now, I think, and last time she came in she said they were moving in together. But that was a couple of years ago. Haven't heard from her since.

Ruby's the opposite. Bless her heart. Hasn't missed a visit—ever. Poppa came with her too, right up to the week he died. I thought maybe Ruby would stop after that, specially since she told me she's got a guy now.

But she still never misses a visit, even though it costs her a pile of jippy. And she gave me something special. Check this out.

Photo of Becky.

Same photo Ruby's got on her little shrine at home, only smaller. Which is cute, cos I can carry it about with me. And I do. You better believe it. Only time it comes out of my pocket is when I want to look at it.

Or at night. When it goes under my pillow.

So that's my life here, Bigeyes. I read, study, see people. Keep busy, keep smart, keep out of trouble. And think. Yeah, I think a lot. And there's one other thing. Something I started doing recently.

Using a knife.

But not in the old way. Come over here, Bigeyes. Check out the shelf.

Three sculptures.

Carved out of wood. With a good old-fashioned blade.

We got this instructor called Arty. Teaches painting and pottery and joinery and stuff in the prison workshop. He's careful who he trusts with the tools. But he seems to be cute with me.

So now I'm back with the knife. And I got to tell you, Bigeyes, it felt strange first time I held it after so many years. But you know what? Moment I started carving, something took over. It was like my hands weren't mine any more.

Just like in the old days. When I used the knife for bad shit. My hands just moved by themselves. And here I found the same thing. But this time it wasn't for bad shit.

It was for something good, something worth doing.

Go on, Bigeyes. Cop a glint. Look close. What do you see? Come on, Bigeyes. You got to see it. Arty says I'm good, says I could be amazing if I keep at it. So surely you must see what these sculptures are?

OK. Yeah, yeah. You got it now. Left to right.

Becky, Mary, Jaz.

Three angels.

Carved out of wood.

35

THEN I GET a new visitor.

No one tells me he's coming or who he is. They just take me through and there he is, sitting in the visit room, waiting. Old gobbo, ancient even. Must be over eighty. I know him straight up.

Only ever saw him once, and that was seven years ago. He was standing by a window, looking out as I ran by. But I'd have recognized him anyway. It's in the face. The mouth, the cheeks, the green eyes. Specially them.

And that other thing. The thing with no name. The thing they all got, the people I love. And she had it. Oh, yeah. You bet.

'You're Mary's brother,' I say. 'You're Jacob.'

He doesn't answer. Just studies me, quiet, slow. He's a bit like Poppa, this gobbo. Takes his time. Got plenty of spit too, like Mary. No question. I can tell. I like him.

Not sure he likes me. He's still checking me close. I wait, take my time too. He goes on watching me, then leans slowly forward.

'Yes, I'm Jacob.'

And there's that dreamy Irish voice. Like music.

He's still not sure of me. I got a feeling he didn't want to come. Which case he's doing this for someone else. And there's only one person that could be. I think of her. Like I so often do. Last time I saw her I told her I love her.

And I meant it.

'Mary was my friend,' I say.

I fix Jacob in the eyes.

'And she always will be.'

His face doesn't move. But something changes in it. Just a small thing. And I know I scored a point.

'She saved my life twice,' I say.

'I know.' He pauses. 'And you tried to save hers by driving to The Crown to warn her when you thought she was in danger. And nearly got yourself killed doing so. I saw it from the window.'

He falls silent.

But I think I scored another point.

He turns away suddenly and coughs. A rough, rasping cough. Doesn't sound good. And when he turns back, I see something else in his face. Something I didn't notice before. I think of Mary and her cancer.

'Yes,' he says quietly. 'I'm not doing so well.'

His eyes tell me not to push this further.

'Can you tell me about Mary?' I say. 'Last I heard she was in a hospice.'

'She died there. Quite peaceful. I was with her right through.'

Jacob coughs again, then goes on.

'They looked after her well. She had no regrets. She was even serene at the end.'

He looks down.

'And it's partly because of you.'

He falls silent again. And I can tell he's struggling inside. Cos he's still not sure of me. And who's to blame him, Bigeyes? Eh? I wouldn't be sure of me if I was him.

I think of Mary.

Beautiful Mary. Brave Mary.

Yeah, brave as you'll ever get.

Remember what she said about getting kidnapped and tortured? All cos of her bitch sister. And then breaking out and running for it. Jesus, she was some woman. Braver than I've ever been. Braver than any of the guys in this prison. And there's some hard dronks in here.

I'm glad she died sweet.

Back in the old city.

Jacob looks up again.

'She talked about you a lot,' he says. 'She worried about you.'

'I didn't want her worrying about me.'

'Neither did I.'

I feel the edge in his voice and look away. A picture floats into my head, of Mary last time I saw her. She was lying in that dronky bed. Weak and ill but full of spirit. I hate to think of her worrying about me when she was dying.

Jacob speaks again.

Like he's picked up my thought.

'She wasn't worrying about you right at the end. Because by then she'd made a decision. And talked me round to it. Which took some doing, I have to admit.'

We fix eyes again.

He goes on, slow.

'Have you given any thought to what you'll do if they ever let you out of here?'

I shrug.

'They won't.'

'You don't know that.'

'Yeah, I do,' I say. 'I'm here for good. And fair enough. I don't deserve to be outside. I'm a danger to society. You got any idea how many guys I killed?'

'I know exactly how many guys you killed. I also know you're no danger to anyone.'

Jacob holds my gaze.

'And I know other things about you too.'

He frowns.

'But I only found out what I really needed to know in the last few minutes.'

He leans back in the chair, still watching me. And for a moment I see Mary's eyes in his, watching me too.

'You might be right,' he says eventually. 'They may never let you out of prison. But I also think it's possible that in ten, twenty, thirty years, whatever, you may find yourself outside with a new name, a new identity and a new start.'

'You got some special information I don't know about?'

Jacob shakes his head.

'I just think it's possible that some years from now they'll give you another chance.'

'Why should they?'

'Because you deserve another chance.'

I watch him close. There was something in that last sentence.

Something he's still fighting. I felt it in the words.

'You don't believe that,' I say.

He doesn't answer. I try again.

'You don't believe I deserve another chance. Not really. You're here cos someone else believed it. Someone special to both of us. And you made a promise to her. And now you're worried you won't be able to honour that promise cos you're ill, cos you're . . . '

I stop. Don't want to say it. But he nods.

'You're right,' he says. 'And you're also wrong.'

He turns away, gives another rasping cough, looks back.

'You're right that it was Mary who believed in you and not me. Even while I was sitting here waiting for you, I didn't want to see you. But I made a promise to Mary, and yes, I'm not going to be around much longer, and I couldn't bear the thought of dying without doing what I told her I would.'

He gives another cough.

'But you're also wrong. Because in the last few minutes I've seen what she saw in you.'

I stare at him.

'But I haven't done anything in the last few minutes. Haven't said anything. Nothing special anyway.'

'It's not about that,' says Jacob. 'It's about . . . just knowing. Knowing when something's right.'

He pauses.

'And I've got a feeling you understand exactly what I mean by that.'

I do, Bigeyes. Christ, I do.

But I say nothing.

He reaches down suddenly, pulls a sheet of paper out of a bag, pushes it over to me. I look down at it. It's a page torn from a recipe book. There's a heading with the words 'Coq au Vin', then a list of ingredients and a description of how to cook it.

I bung a glance at Jacob.

And catch another new thing in his face. The nearest thing I've seen to a smile.

'Other side,' he murmurs.

I turn the page over.

'Mary tore it out of a recipe book at The Crown,' he adds. 'It was all we could find in a hurry.'

And there on the other side is what was once a blank page. Only now it's been covered by a blotty red pen. Handwritten words at the top. Mary's name, address, date of birth, other stuff about her. Then underneath that a heading in capital letters.

BLADE.

And then a written description of what I'm like. Or what I was like when I was fourteen. When I last saw Mary. She's described my face, my hair, everything she can think of. And then she's done a drawing. Or more like a diagram.

And I shudder.

Cos I recognize right away what it is.

She's drawn the wounds on my back. The knife marks I showed her that night in The Crown. Drawn 'em spot on. No wonder she got Jacob to tear a sheet out quick, first thing they could find. She'd want to draw the wounds while she had 'em in her mind.

I look up at Jacob.

'Why this?' I ask.

'She knew so little about you,' he says, 'and she wanted to describe you in as much detail as she could. Because she wanted this paper to be a legal document. Something that could be used to identify both her and you. That's why she signed and dated it at the bottom and had it witnessed by myself and one of the nurses at the hospice.'

He stares down at the paper.

'You're a young man,' he murmurs. 'To someone my age you're a young man. And in ten or twenty or even thirty years, you'll still be a young man. You'll still have a future.'

Another silence.

I swear I hear my heart beating.

Jacob looks up, leans closer.

'During Mary's last few days,' he says, 'she added an expression of wishes to her will. It was something she wanted me to honour. I didn't want to promise it. Certainly not without a stack of conditions. But she wouldn't have it. There were to be no conditions of any kind. All she said to me was . . . '

He lowers his voice.

'Leave the farm to Blade.'

36

THE KNIFE DARTS forward. Flick, twist, jab. It has no thinking behind it. The knife hates thoughts. Thoughts freeze it. So it moves like it's always moved. In its own space. With its own life. And I just watch.

Flick, twist, jab.

Chip, chip, chip.

The block of wood starts to change.

I look round the prison workshop. Just three other inmates. Matti and Tex doing paintings, Dosh trying another pot. He stuffed up the last two. Arty's supervising from the far end. But he looks cool.

Cos none of us is trouble.

Chip, chip, chip.

I turn the block, look it over.

Chip, chip, chip.

Don't know what to feel, Bigeyes. I guess I'm blown away.

Mary, Mary.

I can't believe she did it. And no conditions. Her farm in southern Ireland. Jacob says it's mine the moment he passes away. He's got it sorted, legal-wise. Says there's no complications. Mary's sister Louisa's died. So's her husband.

And the farm's being run by three gobbos Mary used to employ. Close friends of hers. Father and two sons. Honest guys, Jacob says. They know about Mary's last wish and they're going to stay on after Jacob dies. For her sake and his.

And the farm's going to be held in trust for me.

Yeah, Bigeyes.

Trust.

Good word.

Something it's taken me a long time to understand. Jaz used to trust. Remember that time Bex said to me, 'She just trusts,' and I thought how stupid? Cos I reckoned everybody who trusts must be stupid. But that's only cos I didn't know how to trust.

So Jaz taught me. Like Becky did.

And now Mary's done the same.

Jacob says I can do what I like with the farm. Sell it or work it. But I could see the challenge in his face when he said that. And I could feel the word coming at me again through his eyes.

Trust.

Yeah, Bigeyes.

All the way from Mary.

And I'm telling you, I won't betray that trust. If I'm stuck in prison for life, fair enough. I'll crack it best I can. But if I ever get out, I'll make that farm work. I'll do everything I can to persuade those three gobbos to stay on. And teach me what I got to know. They just might come to trust me too. If I can show 'em I learn quick.

And that's one thing I am sure about.

I learn quick.

Chip, chip, chip.

Turn the block, look it over.

Chip, chip, chip.

Got so many emotions running through me, Bigeyes. I never thought I had a future. Didn't reckon I deserved one. Not outside anyway. And maybe it's pie in the sky. Maybe I'm here for good. But even if I never see the farm, I got something else.

Hope.

Cos that's what Mary's really given me.

'Shit!' comes a shout.

I look up from the block of wood. Dosh has screwed up another pot. He's glumming down at the mess. Tex leans round the side of his painting, calls over to him.

'Looks good from here, man.'

'Piss off!'

Tex dissolves. Matti flicks paint at him. I see Arty coming over. He trigs up, stops by me.

'How you doing?' he says.

'OK.'

Chip, chip, chip.

I feel him staring at the block of wood.

'Your wife had her baby yet?' I mutter.

'Not last time I looked.'

Chip, chip, chip.

'What you working on?' he says.

'Come back later.'

He chuckles and trigs back to the others.

Yeah, yeah. So what am I working on, Bigeyes?

More than Arty knows, more than I know. I guess I'm just working on . . . making sense of all this. Cos it still doesn't seem possible they could ever let me out. But Jacob's right about one thing.

I'm no danger to anyone. Haven't been for a very long time. And never will be again. And I guess they know that in here. Cos here's something, Bigeyes. I never wanted to touch a knife again, right? Never went near one in prison.

Till someone stuck a blade in my hand.

Know who that was?

Arty.

He stood next to me, like he did just now, and said go on, mate, try making a sculpture. Here's a block of wood. And then he hands me a knife. And just turns away. Lets me get on with it.

Trust.

Yeah, again.

Chip, chip, chip.

So who's left to hate? Not Hawk. And I don't just mean cos he's dead. I don't hate him anyway. Or his slimehead friends. International porkers cleaned up some of those bastards. I heard it on the news.

Raven, Swift, Condor, some of 'em. Not all. And not Eagle. The Number One. Eagle's still out there. Whoever Eagle is. I just know they haven't nailed that dreg.

So the Game's still alive.

But I'm no part of it any more. I got no further role to play.

Thank Christ.

So yeah, who's left to hate? Hard to say now cos I'm running out of enemies. But there is one left, Bigeyes. One enemy I got to sort. I turn the block of wood again, check it over.

Chip, smooth, brush away the shavings.

Hold it up.

Sound of goony laughter, then footsteps. I look up. They're coming over, all four of 'em.

'What you got, then?' says Matti.

They crowd round, jostling. Only Arty stands back a bit.

Got a quiet smile on his face. And is that just coincidence?

Cos Mary had a smile like that.

'What you got, then?' says Matti again.

I hold up the sculpture, turn the head round so they see the face. They study it gravely.

'That you as a kid?' says Matti eventually.

Dosh sniffs.

'Man, you was one ugly shit.'

'My dog looked better than you,' says Tex. 'And that was when I buried him.'

I cuff him round the head.

Arty leans in, raises my arm so the sculpture moves close to my face. Then gives a nod.

'Good likeness,' he says. 'Even allowing for the difference in age. How old are you meant to be in this sculpture? Six, seven, eight?'

'Seven.'

'That's very precise.'

'Yeah, it is.'

They don't ask any more. But they go on looking.

And not seeing.

I'm glad they don't see. They aren't meant to. Nobody's meant to. I don't want anyone to see who this figure really is. And I don't think anyone ever will. I know it looks like me when I was seven. But it's not me. It's the little boy.

The boy who killed my enemy.

And then disappeared.

I'll never forget him, Bigeyes. And now I got him carved in wood so he can sit there with Becky and Mary and Jaz.

Cos he's an angel too.

The guys break off, back to their work. And I break off, back to my thoughts.

Cos I still haven't answered the question.

Who's left to hate?

Truth is, Bigeyes, there's no one. But like I said earlier, I still got one enemy to sort. I don't hate him, but I want to nail him. Cos he's tough and gritty and clever and he won't go away. Unless I deal with him. So yeah. Just one big enemy left.

ME.

37

NIGHT. PRISON'S QUIET. I love this time.
I like the days cos I keep busy and I'm happy being busy,
but I like the nights even better. Nights are when I lie
awake in my little cell and gaze up, and dream.

Check that out, Bigeyes. The ceiling. All dark and still.

But it's not really a ceiling. Not right now. Right now
it's a big glass dome, like Hawk had in his tower, and I'm
peering through it at the night sky. And it's a big clear sky.
Jesus, it's so clear.

Not a cloud anywhere and stars popping out all over it.
And the funnyface moon glinting down.

Remember that night I spent shivering in a pipe on
that building site? I looked up and saw Orion sparkling
down at me. I got an even better view from here. Check
over the sky, Bigeyes. You name the star, I'll point it out.

I know where they all are.

I learnt 'em.

And now I got 'em. Safe in my head.

Close my eyes, take a slow breath.

Yeah, Bigeyes. I am the last enemy. I'm everything that stands in the way of being the person I should be. I got help everywhere I look. I got Ruby and Bannerman and Dorothea and Trevor and Arty and Dominic and Father Brendan and Jacob, and all kinds of other nebs behind me.

And I got my angels to inspire me.

But the past still slams in. The flashbacks and nightmares keep coming. I hoped they might ease up but they don't. Father Brendan says they probably never will go. Not total. I got to accept 'em, he reckons. He also says I got to forgive myself.

I know he's right. Cos there's someone in the way. And that person's me. I want to nail that last enemy. I want to forgive him. But I need your help, Bigeyes. Cos I can't do this on my own.

Open my eyes. Look over at the shelf.

My angels sit quietly watching. Reach under my pillow, pull out Becky's photo, hold it close, look up at the dream sky, the dream moon, the dream stars.

Think back, Bigeyes. Right back.

Cos I got a question for you.

How come I only started talking to you when I was fourteen? Eh? Cos I didn't before that. I didn't even know you were there. I just . . . crashed through my life and messed up and . . . never even knew about you.

Till I was fourteen.

So what happened when I was fourteen? Did you come looking for me? Cos I don't remember looking for you. Maybe we came looking for each other. Without even knowing it.

But I'll tell you something, Bigeyes.

First time we talked I said I didn't like people getting close, remember? And I said that included you. Well, it did back then. I wasn't ready to talk. Not even to you. But now? I'm glad you're there, Bigeyes. I really am. I'm glad I can talk to you. I just wanted to tell you that.

Not that you don't still piss me off sometimes. Even after all these years. Specially when I screw up something. Cos that's the time when I don't want anyone knowing what I've done. And there you are, gawping at me.

I hated that in the beginning. I wanted you around, yeah. But only on my terms. It's different now, honest. Cos here's something I've learned. About you seeing everything.

That's your strength. And if I can just deal with it, then it's my strength too. Not worrying about you knowing. Good or bad, no bum gripe. Cos there's another strength you got. And I really like this one.

You don't judge me.

I wish I had that strength but I don't. I judge all the time. I can feel myself doing it. Dosh splats up his pot and I'm thinking what a dimp. How difficult can it be to make a pot? And then I feel you watching me. Not judging, just watching.

And I kind of learn something myself. About watching, not judging.

So why? Eh, Bigeyes? Why didn't we meet earlier? You know what I think? I think we were meant to meet but I had to be ready. Simple as that. I had to be ready. And I was. Took me till I was fourteen, but I got there in the end.

Maybe I'm right, maybe I'm wrong.

But there's one thing I am clear about.

We're never going to be apart, Bigeyes. No messing. You and me. We're in this together. For good. Don't ask me how I know. But I'm cool about it. Oh, yeah. I wouldn't want it any other way.

Cos I can't imagine a life now without you in it.

I kiss Becky's photo. Look at my angels.

Look at the night sky.

Makes me think of that bit in *The Wind in the Willows*. When Ratty and Mole go off in their boat under the moonlight. They've heard their mate Otter's little kid's gone missing so they go looking for him. They row down the river towards this island, cos they got a feeling he might be somewhere there.

And as they get close, the dawn starts breaking. And they hear this soft music in the air. And they're kind of scared and excited at the same time. Cos they know there's something strange and mysterious and beautiful close by. They can feel it but they don't know what it is. But they row on and moor the boat and trig off over the island.

And find the little otter fast asleep.

And then they have this vision.

Of a big friendly spirit watching over 'em.

Right there, on the island.

And everything's plum, Bigeyes. They're scared and confused and they feel weak and vulnerable, but everything's plum. I used to dream of that vision. In my snugs, when I was curled up on someone else's bed, trying to sleep, I used to pretend I was the little otter, lying there.

With a big friendly spirit watching over me.

And dawn breaking.

I kiss Becky's photo again.

I'll settle for what I got, Bigeyes.

My memories, my angels, my future.

My big friendly spirit.

My dawn breaking.

And you. Sweet friend.

I'll settle for you.

Tim Bowler is one of the UK's most compelling and original writers for teenagers. He was born in Leigh-on-Sea and after studying Swedish at university, he worked in forestry, the timber trade, teaching and translating before becoming a full-time writer. He lives with his wife in a small village in Devon and his workroom is an old stone outhouse known to friends as 'Tim's Bolthole'.

Tim has written eighteen books and won fifteen awards, including the prestigious Carnegie Medal for *River Boy*, and his provocative *BLADE* series is being hailed as a groundbreaking work of fiction. He has been described by the *Sunday Telegraph* as 'the master of the psychological thriller' and by the *Independent* as 'one of the truly individual voices in British teenage fiction'.

The complete
Blade collection

TIM BOWLER
winner of the carnegie medal

ENEMIES

I'm called Blade
for a reason.
Remember that.

Book one in the BLADE series

TIM BOWLER
winner of the carnegie medal

FLIGHT

I'm called Blade
for a reason.
Remember that.

Book two in the BLADE series

TIM BOWLER
winner of the carnegie medal

FIRESTORM

I'm called Blade
for a reason.
Remember that.

Book three in the BLADE series

TIM BOWLER
winner of the carnegie medal

ENDGAME

I'm called Blade
for a reason.
Remember that.

Book four in the BLADE series